Love Practice

A GOOD BAD IDEA NOVEL

ARIELLA ZOELLE

Copyright © 2021 A.F. Zoelle/Ariella Zoelle

Published by Sarayashi Publishing

www.ariellazoelle.com

All rights reserved.

This is a work of fiction. Names, characters, places, and incidents are products of the author's imagination or used fictitiously. Any resemblance to actual persons, living or dead, is purely coincidental. All products and brand names are registered trademarks of their respective holders/companies.

This book or any portion thereof may not be reproduced or used in any manner whatsoever without the express written permission of the publisher except for the use of brief quotations in a book review.

Cover Design by Cate of Cate Ashwood Designs

Editing by Pam of Undivided Editing

Proofreading by Sandra of One Love Editing

Layout by Ariella of Sarayashi Publishing

ISBN: 978-1-954202-02-3

Author's Note

The **Good Bad Idea** series can be read in any order. However, if you would like to see where Wren and Izzy's story began, please refer to **Love Means More**. They also appears in Chapter 3 of **Fancy Love** and in **Picture Love**. This book starts three months after the epilogue of the previous book.

Dedication

This book is for all of my wonderful readers who changed my life for the better this past year.

Welcome to Sunnyside

Immerse yourself in the world of interconnected series set in Sunnyside!

Full of cute sweetness and sexy fun, every story ends with a satisfying HEA and no cliffhangers. Since all of the following series are set in the same town, you can expect to see cameos of some of your favorite characters! The books are funny, steamy, and can be read in any order.

To access the Sunnyside universe reading order guide, please visit www.ariellazoelle.com/sunnyside

Chapter One

WREN

WHY WAS FINDING true love so hard? All I wanted was to find the perfect man whose dick I could suck for the rest of my life. What guy wouldn't want to sign up for a lifetime of love, blow jobs, and fucking me into the mattress when I was cute as hell?

After yet another disaster of a first date, I came home to my apartment and gave in to the temptation to slam the door shut behind me with frustration. It made me feel marginally better about my shitty night.

My best friend and roommate, Izzy, looked up from his reading on the couch. He looked like a handsome prince from a fairy tale, with a regal bearing to match. In black skinny jeans and a white sweater with the sleeves pushed up, he was the perfect image of a royal trying to play the part of a commoner.

He arched one of his annoyingly perfect eyebrows

at me as he asked in his sexy French accent, "Another bad date, eh?"

I dropped onto the couch next to him with a huff. "It wasn't my fault this time!"

Izzy set his book aside to give me his full attention. "Are you sure about that?"

"When Trevor found out I'm vegetarian, he said he could never be with someone who didn't eat meat. I made a joke about being fine with enjoying his man meat, and he got offended." I scowled when my best friend rolled his eyes with a heavy sigh. "He's the one who had his sense of humor surgically removed, yet somehow *I'm* the problem?"

"I suppose the bright side is at least you found out early on that your special brand of uncouth humor was wasted on him."

Crossing my arms with a pout, I threw myself back against the couch. "Can I ask a dumb question?"

"Better than anyone I know."

I ignored the dig, heaving a defeated sigh. "What's wrong with me?"

Izzy didn't hesitate to answer. "You're a chronic procrastinator thanks to your perfectionism. That in turn feeds off your lack of self-confidence. Plus, you have a deep need to please everyone so they'll like you."

"Wow, I'm *so* glad to see your Psych 101 class really paid off. Looks like that four-hundred-dollar textbook was worth it after all." I threw a pillow at him for good measure.

"Hey, I'm not wrong," he said with a laugh, blocking it from hitting him in his perfect face. *Jerk.*

"No, you're not." I scowled in irritation. "Fine, why can't I make it to a second date?"

"Maybe if you were more selective about who you went out with instead of accepting everyone you match with on a dating app, you would have better results."

I considered what he suggested. "You're saying my issue is that I should stop going for quantity and start aiming for quality?"

"*Oui.*"

It was a fair point. "That isn't my only problem, though."

"True. I believe you are what North calls 'too thirsty' to find a boyfriend," Izzy said.

"Well, excuse me for wanting to be with someone who wants to fuck me into oblivion all the time."

He gave me a patronizing look. "Oh, poor *bébé.*"

"If you'd just give in to the sexual tension between us, we'd both be much happier." I was only half-joking. We'd built our whole friendship on me flirting with Izzy and him shooting me down.

"While you think that's the answer to everything, it won't fix your problems, *mon ami.*"

"Come on, you'd love to shut me up by making me suck your dick."

He smirked at me. "We both know that wouldn't make you silent."

"It's worth a shot." I gave him my best puppy dog eyes. "May I pretty please blow you instead of jerking off all by my lonesome tonight?"

"*Non*, I think not."

I pouted over being denied, despite it being the answer I expected. "Just imagine how hilarious my shocked reaction would be if you said '*oui*' to me. That would definitely make me speechless."

"Your efforts would be better spent on getting a real boyfriend."

"Yeah, but I'm not having any luck with finding one of those. At this point, I'd settle for a fuck buddy." I made another pass at him for the fun of it. "You're already my buddy, so we just need the fucking part to make it happen."

"You don't mean that."

"Oh, I definitely do." I fidgeted on the couch as I struggled with my horniness. "It's been like two months since I've been able to enjoy myself to the fullest. I'm dying."

"You're so dramatic."

"I can't find a soul mate, a boyfriend, or a dude who wants to rail me for a night. I'm allowed to be a drama queen about it." I moved to straddle his lap, looping my arms around his neck with a sultry expression. Rather than hugging me like I wanted, he reacted by draping one arm over the back of the couch and kept his other on the armrest. "A good, deep-dicking from you is what we both need tonight."

He laughed at my attempt to seduce him. "*Non*, you're not getting in my bed."

"You can fuck me on the floor, then. I'm not picky."

"*Pardon*, but I refuse to be your consolation prize for a bad date."

His comment made me grow serious. "Iz, that's not what this is about. Sorry, I was trying to make myself feel better, not upset you."

He looked at me skeptically. "To console yourself about being rejected by Trevor, you need me to turn you down, too? What sense does that make?"

"I'm used to *you* telling me no." I shrugged, not really understanding it myself. "I don't know. It's like restoring my equilibrium when you do it."

He shook his head. "I'll never comprehend how your mind works."

"Wow, Monsieur Know-it-all admitting he doesn't understand something?" I gasped in mock astonishment. "Why, I never!"

"*Très* cute, Wren."

"Yes, I am. How kind of you to notice." I laughed at my joke as he snorted in amusement. "You'd think it would help me land more second dates. Considering how many first dates I go on, I should statistically do better than this. Of course, knowing you, I'm sure you have a list of reasons why I keep striking out."

Izzy didn't disappoint me. "For starters, you have a tendency to come on too strong." He gestured at me, sitting on his lap in a loose embrace as evidence.

Instead of being offended by his accuracy, it inspired me. "That just gave me an idea!"

"Oh no," he groaned.

I shoved at his shoulder. "No, this one is good!"

He didn't look convinced. "Define 'good.'"

"I've come up with a genius plan to use your brilliance to help me!"

"Your definition of 'good' and mine are very different."

My plan excited me the more I thought about it. "No, this is perfect. You should be my dating tutor!"

"Your what?"

"Since you always have an answer for everything and love telling me what I'm doing wrong, this is genius! You can coach me on how to get better at it!"

It was a surprise not to receive a flat-out rejection. "Are you saying that you want me to go on practice dates with you and critique you?"

"Yeah!"

"And what's in it for *moi*?"

I tried to come up with something that would sway him. "The pleasure of my company?"

"I get enough of that as your roommate."

"Come on, is telling me I'm wrong not enough of a draw for you? If you help me practice, I'll get better. Then, I'll have a boyfriend to give me all the sex I want without ending up in your lap, unsuccessfully begging to be fucked."

He scoffed. "I find that hard to believe when being with Joon didn't prevent you from flirting with me."

"I'll never quit doing that because it's too much fun. If we stopped flirting, I'd think you weren't my friend anymore." The mere thought of it hurt my heart.

"Nothing would ever make me stop being your friend."

It was hard not to coo at the rare showing of Izzy's softer side. "There's only one reason I can come up with that would make you refuse to be my dating teacher."

"And what's that?"

"You're scared of falling in love with me for real."

His sexy haughtiness was on full display as he tilted his head. "Don't be absurd."

"So you'll do it?"

"Would you listen to my advice if I did?"

It seemed like I was making some progress. "As long as it isn't something impossible like 'don't be you,' then yeah."

He continued mulling it over. "And we would go on fake dates so you could practice being better at them in the future?"

I shifted in his lap as I leaned closer. "I'll even be a gentleman and buy you dinner as a thank-you."

He was silent for a long pause, making me wonder if he would turn me down. To my great relief, he caved. "Fine. I'm willing to try your little experiment for at least one date."

"Thank you!" I hugged him tight, melting into his hold when he returned the embrace.

Izzy sighed like I annoyed him, but I could hear the amusement in his voice as he asked, "You're not going to move, are you?"

I clung to him tighter. "Not until you make me or I'm in danger of getting a boner."

He laughed, which gratified my ego. "You are hopeless, *mon ami*."

"The word you're looking for is 'incorrigible,' actually."

"That, too."

Since he was in an indulgent mood, I stayed put. He always shot down my passes, but he never turned me away when I needed him. "Thanks for putting up with me."

"I'm the one who should say '*merci beaucoup*' for keeping things so interesting."

Because I was me, I couldn't resist. "Is that an invitation for me to spice up your evening with a lap dance?"

"Is there some reason you're determined to see how many ways you can embarrass yourself tonight?"

I pulled back to tease him a little. "Oh, I get it. You're afraid I'll turn you on if I do it."

"If that's what you have to tell yourself to sleep, sure."

Getting off him instead of getting off with him sucked. "I guess I'll have to settle for jerking off alone in the shower tonight. Unless you want to join me?"

He dismissed me with a wave. "*Non*, I wouldn't want to interfere and make your right hand jealous."

"How considerate of you." I shrugged with a grin. "Anyway, I'm off to celebrate my victory of getting you to agree with a lonely solo night. Come find me if you change your mind."

He laughed as I headed into my room to grab pajamas and my towel before heading into our shared bathroom. I didn't lock the door on the unlikely chance he decided to shock the hell out of me. Dropping my stuff next to the shower, I turned on the water and stripped out of my outfit.

I studied myself in the mirror as I waited for the water to get hot. My neon pink hair had faded to a bubblegum pastel color, which made my boyish features cuter than normal. With my blue eyes, adorable smile, dimples, fun personality, and how much I loved sucking dick, it shouldn't have been so hard to find a man to love me.

Getting into the shower, I hurried through washing my hair. By the time I finished, my cock was already standing at full attention in anticipation of what I was about to do.

It didn't escape me how weird my flirty dynamic

was with Izzy. My inner masochist thrived on the back-and-forth game we played with each other. The more brutal the rejection, the happier it made me. It was probably fucked-up that I enjoyed being shot down by him, but it was so much fun bantering with him. I loved being the center of his attention, even when he was denying me. My idea of a perfect night would be having him edge me until I sobbed for relief, then pound me into the mattress until we both came. The best thing would be cuddling for hours afterward.

...okay, so I might have been a *tiny* bit in love with my best friend for real. Not that it did me any good. However, instead of getting down about him not being the least bit interested in me like that, I chose to ignore that inconvenient part of my heart.

Since I couldn't resist temptation, I poured some of his fancy French bodywash into my palm, filling the shower with its fragrant peach scent. Using it to bathe myself, I then slicked my erection with it as I worked my length while fantasizing about my best friend.

I traced the path of the vein on the underside of Izzy's dick before sucking on the head with a soft moan at getting a taste of him. Focusing on teasing it with my tongue, I drew it into my mouth again.

He stared down at me with an arrogance that made me ache. "Is that the best you can do, Wren?"

His question brought out my competitiveness. With great relish, I started working his cock, taking in more of him with each bob of my head. I didn't stop until he was hitting the back of my throat.

He ran his fingers through my hair in a gentle caress before using the grip to fuck himself in my mouth. I moaned as he used me to get off, turned on by him dominating me in such a way.

When I reached down to touch myself, the bastard pulled out. "Is this not enough pleasure for you?"

"No, so hurry up and take me," I whimpered.

He knocked me flat on my back and pressed the head of his cock at my entrance to tease me with a hint of penetration. "Like this?"

"No, fuck me like you hate me." I groaned when any attempt at forcing him into me failed.

"I could never hate you, mon ami.*"*

"That's why I said like *you do. Please, give it to me quick and dirty, I'm begging you."*

Unlike in real life, Izzy gave me exactly what I wanted as he pounded me hard, his nails digging into my skin as he made me see stars.

I lost myself in the pleasure until he asked, "How many fake dates will it take before you ask me to practice fucking?"

"I'll answer that after I judge your reaction to me asking to rehearse kissing first."

He laughed as he continued drilling me into the mattress. "You know I see straight through you, right?"

"Yeah, because I'm as subtle as a cat in heat. But you agreed anyway, so we're both aware of what game we're playing here."

When he slowed down to more shallow thrusts, I hooked

my ankles behind his ass to force him into me. "Nope, I'm not in the mood for that. I'm dying to come, not play games."

He scoffed at my claim. "Since when?"

"Please, Iz, I'm begging you to get me off."

His answer came in the form of pushing in and coming inside me.

I shot my load all over my hand with a stifled moan. It felt good, but part of me was still unsatisfied. Probably because I hadn't brought a dildo in with me to make my fantasy more realistic. But after I accidentally broke a shower tile off the wall last time thanks to a *very* effective suction cup base, I hesitated to try it again. Thank god I was klutzy enough that Izzy and our building manager bought my "slipped in the shower and knocked a tile off" excuse for the damage. It also helped that our apartment was showing its age by falling apart on the regular, meaning we had legit reasons to put in so many maintenance calls. Thankfully, Arnold was awesome about fixing everything without asking too many questions.

After washing off, I got out, toweled off, and dried my hair. When I finished, I put on my pink T-shirt and black Christmas sweater skull-and-hearts pajama pants, then went back out to the living room.

Izzy was still reading where I had left him. Without glancing up from his book, he asked, "How was your shower?"

"You were great, thanks." I blew him a kiss when he looked up at me, earning me a chuckle. Unable to resist, I lay down on the couch to rest my head in his lap. "I have energy for round two if you're interested."

"That's considerate of you to offer, but *non*." I could see his nostrils flare slightly as he inhaled deeply, catching on to my naughtiness. "Using my bodywash to pleasure yourself again, eh?"

Because I was shameless, I admitted the truth. "It makes my fantasies of us hooking up more realistic."

"Could you not?"

"Hey, if you fucked me for real, I wouldn't be reduced to using your shower gel to get myself off. This is on you."

Izzy snorted in disbelief. "We both know you would still do that no matter what."

"True, but then it would be less creepy." To distract him, I reached up and stole his book. The cover featured a beautiful illustration of a lone male figure standing in a field with a sword. "Is this the French version of Arrietty Quenby's *The Prince's Thief?*"

"*Oui*. Linda asked me to let her know what I thought of the translation." She was North's mom, who was famous for her fantasy novels. The romance between Riston and Hedley was sexy as hell. I had gotten myself off to enough fantasies of the two of them together over the years.

"That's one of my favorites of hers." Giving it back to Izzy, I asked, "Would you read it to me?"

A smile tugged at his lush lips as he looked down at me. "Like a bedtime story?"

"Yeah." I pulled the blanket off the back of the sofa behind us to cover myself up and snuggle against him.

Because he was the best, he started reading out loud without complaint. I closed my eyes as I listened, losing myself in his beautiful voice and the melodious rhythm of him speaking French. It got better when he absentmindedly stroked my hair like I was a kitten as he continued. The moment was so peaceful, even I couldn't ruin it by getting horny. Instead, I drifted into a deep sleep.

I WAS VAGUELY aware of being moved, but I was too sleepy to fight it. Placed into bed, I snuggled into the comforts of it as the covers were pulled over me. The gentle press of tender lips on my forehead melted my heart. In my beautiful fantasy, it was Izzy tucking me in and giving me a good-night kiss like my perfect fairy-tale prince. My dreams were the only place I could be completely honest with myself about how I was deeply in love with my best friend. I wanted to stay asleep forever, instead of waking up in a world where Izzy didn't love me back.

Chapter Two

IZZY

BEING in love with your best friend wasn't wonderfully romantic like in the Hollywood movies. It was a special hell since Wren was a notorious flirt who made overt passes at every possible opportunity. He *constantly* tempted me with what I wanted most but could never have. Continually rejecting the person I loved was fucked-up, even by my standards. But how could I ever accept his playful offers of sexual gratification when he was only joking?

I ached for him to be mine, but that was impossible when he was going out with different men, trying to find a soul mate. A mere fling with him would never satisfy me when I wanted to love him with all my heart. It frustrated me to no end that he couldn't see me standing right in front of him. But it was my fault for shooting him down whenever he flirted with me. When I denied him every time, he'd never believe

I desired him more than life itself. However, if I didn't turn him down, he wouldn't come back for more teasing. I deserved an Oscar for acting like his flirtatious attention annoyed me when everything in me was ready to beg him to keep playing the game with me.

Wren stood in our kitchen, holding the doors to the cabinets open with a scowl at its offerings. I watched him over the edge of my book from the living room couch. His pastel pink hair made his soft features extra cute. It presented an interesting contrast with the fact that most of his wardrobe featured skulls, albeit with heart eyes. It was one of the many adorable things about him I had to pretend not to notice.

Today's T-shirt had two dandelions made of colorful Day of the Dead sugar skulls, some of them floating away in the wind. There were smaller dandelions with red hearts as the perfect finishing touch with his hot pink pants. It was so perfectly Wren.

He sighed dramatically while squirming in front of the doors with an indecisive noise. Whenever he became stressed, small decisions overwhelmed him, especially regarding food. It was something he beat himself up about when his anxiety was too much for him. I hated watching him be so unkind to himself when he loved everyone else with all his heart. He was stubborn and proud, so I always did my part to help him without him being aware of what I was doing.

Setting my book aside, I raised my voice so he

would hear me. "Has our food offended your delicate sensibilities again?"

"I know I need to eat lunch, but nothing sounds good." He pouted at me over his shoulder, tugging at my heart.

Early in our friendship, I used to suggest options to help him, but I had learned that overwhelmed him even more because there were too many choices. It was much easier to decide for him to take away the struggle of having to make up his mind while still letting him save face. "I'm ordering something from Cavatolli's for lunch. Do you want your usual?" He was a creature of habit who always ordered only his favorite meal at a restaurant, so I knew all his preferences by heart.

"Yeah! Great idea." As I placed an order from my phone, Wren came over and flopped onto the couch next to me, cuddling up against my side. "Thank you."

I smothered my urge to pull him closer and wrap him up in my embrace. "You're welcome, *mon ami*."

He nuzzled against me, which did nothing to quell my desires. "It's so hot when you take charge. I bet you do that in bed, too." He moaned as he shifted next to me, giving me perverse thoughts I wasn't allowed to have. "Fuck, it makes me wish you would pin me down and dominate the hell out of me."

"You are many things, but submissive is not one of them."

Wren pulled back to grin at me with boyish glee. "Maybe I put up a fight to make it more exciting for you. Did you ever think of that?"

It was true I liked my men with some fire in them, which was why I was so drawn to my best friend. "*Touché.*"

"That reminds me. When are we going on our first practice date?"

"You have yet to ask me out."

He tilted his head as he gave me an adorably confused look. "Sure I did. I asked you on a date, and you agreed."

"Asking if I would give you dating advice is different from asking me out."

He made a show of formally requesting, "Will you please go on a fake date with me?"

"If that's how you ask, it's no wonder you can't get a second one," I said with a grin. "Would you really ask someone point-blank like that?"

"No, but it's you."

"Consider this your first lesson, then. Pretend I'm a stranger you're asking out."

He furrowed his eyebrows at me. "But I have no problem with getting the first date. It's the second one that's the issue."

"It's good practice for when you aren't relying on swiping right to go out with someone. Try acting like this is the first time you've ever spoken to me."

Eager to please, he got off the couch to approach

me with a little wave. When he came closer, shyness replaced his normal brash demeanor. It was utterly charming. "Um, hey. I'm Wren from Professor Carrigan's class."

He reached out to shake hands, but it was too tempting to tease him. I took his hand in mine, then brought it up to my lips to kiss while gazing up at him with a seductive expression. "*Enchanté*, Wren. My name is Isidore, but you can call me Izzy."

His cheeks flushed as he stared at me with wide eyes, trembling in my hold. "Holy fuck, it should be illegal to be that sexy. Stop it."

"*Pardon.*"

"Bullshit, you're not sorry at all. I hope you're happy that I'm dying to jump in your lap and make out with you now."

It took an epic show of willpower not to invite him to give in to that desire. "You seem to have forgotten that I'm supposed to be a stranger."

He scowled at me. "That's because you short-circuited my brain by being all seductive. All I want right now is to get on my knees and suck your dick."

"What *doesn't* make you want to do that?" I asked him with an arched eyebrow.

"Good point." His wolfish grin made me laugh.

"Do I need to remind you what your goal is?"

He raked his fingers through his spiky hair. "Nope, I'm still laser focused on getting in your pants."

I rolled my eyes. "You have no hope of that without asking me out on a date first."

"Okay, okay. I've got this." He exhaled as he drew his finger into a point like an actor preparing for a scene. "Mind if I join you?"

I gestured for him to take a seat, biting the inside of my lip to keep myself from laughing at him predictably sitting closer than was necessary.

"You always bring up a lot of interesting points in class, so I'd enjoy the chance to get to know you better. Do you want to grab lunch together sometime?"

I rewarded him for making a genuine effort. "Are you free now? I was about to go to Cavatolli's. It's a great Italian restaurant that's not too far from here."

"Yeah, that sounds awesome! Thanks." He gave me a brilliant smile that reminded my heart of how in love with him I was. "So, how'd I do?"

"You didn't embarrass yourself."

He laughed as he rested his elbow on the back of the couch. "Hey, I'll take it. That's no small feat for me."

"True."

"Does this mean lunch will be our first date?"

"That depends. Would you consider that a date or only dinner?"

He stroked his chin as he thought about his answer. "Good point." A smile tugged at his lips. "Do

I get bonus points for being more appropriate during practice than I was the first time I met you?"

"Sure." I chuckled at the reminder as the scene replayed in my mind from when Wren had crashed into my life during freshman orientation week in a literal sense.

A guy with electric-blue hair caught my attention as I walked back to my dorm. He wore a shirt decorated with a skull and crossbones that had hearts for eyes and a pink crown that said "Pastel Goth Princess" paired with lavender pants. His sharp cheekbones, full lips, and boyish features stood out as particularly beautiful. When we made eye contact, a spark ignited within me that turned into a roaring blaze. It startled me when he stumbled right into my path.

I caught him on instinct. As long as I lived, I'd never forget the awed way he whispered, "Wow."

For some reason, it was impossible to release him. I kept my arm around his waist as I held his smaller body against mine in a loose embrace. It was hard to find my voice to ask, "Are you okay?"

His radiant smile did things to my heart I didn't understand. "Better than okay. I'm the second luckiest man in the world."

"The second *luckiest man? Who's the first?"*

"You."

I arched an eyebrow at him. "Why do you say that?"

He wrapped his arms around me in a hug as he grinned up at me. "Because you just met me."

It was so absurd I had to laugh. "Is that so?"

"Yep. According to the rules of romance, we're destined to fall in love thanks to this meet-cute. That makes you the luckiest man in the universe because I'm fucking awesome."

"You're certainly something." There was something magical about him, which was the only way to explain why I was fine hugging a total stranger.

"I'm your new best friend and future husband."

When he used a pickup line like that, it amazed me he appeared charming and not obnoxious. "You say that with a shocking amount of confidence considering you don't know my name yet."

"I bet it's something sexy I'm going to love to moan."

It was hard not to laugh. "Are you always this way?"

"Yep, so you better get used to it." His cheeky smirk made him even cuter somehow. "Now, tell me what name I get to call out as you pleasure me."

"Isidore Devereaux."

The way he gasped my first name like I was moving inside him was seared into my mind forever. It filled me with a burning need to take him up on his offer. "Ooh, I love it. I'm definitely getting the better end of the deal with names, though."

"Why?"

"Because Wren isn't sexy at all," he said with an adorable pout. "I mean, it's better than Alfred, but it won't rank on the Top 100 list of the sexiest names to cry out during sex."

His playfulness brought out the shameless flirt in me. I caressed under his chin as I tipped his head back for a better glimpse at him. His long eyelashes and thin eyebrows were so blond they were almost white, giving him an ethereal appearance.

"Non, *I disagree.*" *To prove my point, I moaned his name in a sensuous rumble.*

The lust burning bright in his eyes thrilled me. "Well, that settles it."

"Settles what?"

"You're stuck with me now," *he declared.* "Let's grab dinner and get to know each other better."

*What else could I say other than "*Oui*" to an offer from such an enthralling person?*

It took an effort to refocus myself on the present moment. "Most people would not react well to you proposing during your first encounter."

"That's why you're my best friend and they aren't," he said with a shrug.

A knock interrupted us. Wren went over to answer the door and get our food while I grabbed drinks and silverware for us to bring to the table. He scowled as he put the bag down and started unloading it.

"What's wrong, Wren?"

"I'm such a dumbass. I was supposed to be treating you, but you paid since you ordered on your phone."

"You said you would be a gentleman and treat me to dinner. This is lunch." I sat down and opened the container to reveal my chicken marsala. "Consider it your reward for taking practice somewhat seriously."

He grinned at me as he ate his four-cheese medallion ravioli in vodka sauce. "In that case, does that mean I don't have to be a gentleman during lunch?"

"Are you ever capable of being one?"

"Hey, I can be a classy gent if I want to be." He straightened his posture with an arrogant tilt of his head, speaking with a posh British accent. "Shall I prove it by espousing my erudite critiques of psychosexual impulses amongst the upper echelon of pulchritudinous males?"

Wren had a fascinating ability to humor and arouse me like no one else ever had. "What kind of males?"

"Pulchritudinous."

My English was excellent, but I was unfamiliar with that word. "Which means?"

"It's an esoteric term for 'beautiful' that proves I am a gentleman with a predilection for aesthetically prepossessing beaus." He gave a disdainful sniff, but I could see how hard he was struggling not to break character.

"And you know this why?"

"For your edification, it's because I've been inculcated in the ivory tower by the foremost gatekeepers of pedagogical tutelage."

I took a bite of my lunch to stop myself from laughing. "Forgive me for being unaware I was in the presence of such an illustrious elite."

Wren lost his battle against his amusement, and his haughtiness dissolved into an adorable giggle fit. "My parents will be *so* proud those SAT prep classes finally paid off. God, pretentious fuckers like that are the *worst*."

"I much prefer you as you are now."

He propped his chin on his hand as he batted his eyelashes at me. "Aww, you say the sweetest things." His expression turned sensuous in a way that caused me to shift in my seat. "But wouldn't you prefer me naked and in your bed instead?"

It was everything I wanted but would never happen. "You should be so lucky."

I expected him to continue teasing me about the subject, but he surprised me by pivoting into a different one. "Who is?"

"What do you mean?"

"Who's lucky enough to be in your bed?"

Questions like that made me wish Wren believed in personal boundaries sometimes. I didn't want to answer, so I did my best to distract him. "Are you questioning my credentials as your dating tutor?"

He shrugged. "Not really. I'm curious, because you don't go out like you used to, and you don't bring anyone over anymore."

"You just answered your own question."

My response didn't satisfy him. "But that's such a waste!"

It had not been the protest I expected. "Would you prefer me to entertain myself with other men instead of helping you?"

He had that faraway gleam in his eyes he got every time he fantasized. I could only imagine who he was imagining me fucking in his mind. "It depends on who it is and if you'd let me watch."

"You should finish your lunch rather than think about such things."

"It's your fault for being so mysterious. Plus, Arsène dropped that tantalizing tidbit at dinner last week about your sexual adventures in Paris, so spill it."

While I was close to my older brother, I had wanted to kill him for making that comment in front of Wren. My best friend's overactive imagination would go supernova if he knew about that part of my life. Thanks to Arsène's career as a world-famous photographer, his studio was always full of celebrities and models. Since I worked for him during breaks from school, I had hooked up with a few over the years.

On my visit home the previous summer, I'd had a tryst with Rook Warrick, a closeted man who also was one of Wren's favorite A-list Hollywood actors. If he ever found out that I had enjoyed a week of the best sex of my life with Rook, I'd never hear the end of it. Despite how satisfying my no-strings-attached time with him had been, it hadn't helped me stop loving my roommate.

I pushed my thoughts aside and dismissively waved my hand. "It's not worth talking about."

"Why? Did you hook up with a celebrity that required you sign an NDA?" At my puzzled look,

Wren clarified what he meant. "Non-disclosure agreement. It means you're contractually bound not to talk about something."

"*Non*, I have never signed such a document."

He seized on the technicality in my denial. "But you have hooked up with someone famous?"

There wasn't a chance in hell I was going to give him a new fantasy for his self-proclaimed "spank bank." I took a long sip of my drink to avoid answering right away. "Why don't you put that vivid imagination of yours to better use by thinking about our dinner date, eh?"

"I swear to god, if you've fucked someone hot like Rook Warrick, Kieran Aiello, or Iason Leyland and didn't tell me, you're going to be in *so* much trouble later on." His playful threat made me stiffen at his accuracy at guessing one of my previous sexual partners. "So, is our date supposed to be fancy, or can we go to one of our regular places?"

"That's up to you."

He continued eating as he considered his options. "What about that place near Rune and Callum's apartment where Red works? We haven't been there in a while."

"The Hurly-burly Bar? Sure."

"Sorry in advance if I keep fucking up by forgetting to treat you like a stranger. I'm not used to having to be on my best behavior with you."

Considering it was something that amused me

rather than annoyed me, it was no trouble. "I'm sure you'll do your best. And who knows? Perhaps you might find out something about me you didn't know before."

"Like which sexy celebrity you've nailed?"

His question was a reminder to talk to my brother about his faux pas. "A gentleman never kisses and tells."

"As long as you're a gentleman on the streets and a freak in the sheets, that's fine."

It was impossible not to laugh at his silliness. Even if we were only friends, he was still the bright spot in my universe. I ignored the gloomy storm cloud hanging over my heart that reminded me of an uncomfortable fact. By teaching Wren how to get better at dates, I was also helping him be with someone who wasn't me. It made me a terrible person for wanting him to learn how to fall in love with me as I taught him about dating. But it gave me a glimmer of sunshine to keep me going with such a foolish plan. After all, I knew my best friend and what he needed better than anyone. Somehow, I had to help him understand I was what was best for him and not just a perverse punchline to joke about.

Chapter Three

WREN

AS SOON AS I arrived at the Hurly-burly Bar and Grille, I went straight to the bar to get something to calm myself. It was ridiculous I was nervous about going on a practice date with my best friend, but my anxiety had always been a pain in the ass.

Thankfully, my favorite bartender was working tonight. Red was hella cute and fun to flirt with, plus he made the best cocktails ever. With fiery auburn hair, green eyes, and an easygoing personality, he was a blast to talk to. It was a bonus that he looked damn fine in his bartender's uniform of a black vest over his white button-down shirt and jeans.

I hopped up on one of the barstools as I waved at him. "Hey, Red!"

"Welcome back. It's been so long since you've been here, I was starting to think you didn't like me anymore."

"Nah, you're still my favorite bartender," I said. "I've just been slammed with school and chasing guys."

Red laughed as he pulled out a tall glass. "Have you had any luck catching one?"

"Nope. Apparently, my sparkling personality is too much to handle."

"Well, they're stupid and doing you a favor by taking themselves out of your dating pool." He began making my favorite blue lagoon. It was a pretty cocktail that combined lemonade, Curacao, and vodka on ice with a garnish of cherries, a lemon slice, and a pink umbrella. "Are you meeting a date tonight, or are you hanging out with your friends?"

I accepted the drink as he passed it over to me. That was the great thing about having a favorite bartender; he knew what to make without me having to ask for anything. "Technically both."

He leaned against the counter with a wicked grin. "Good for you. It's about time you and Izzy got together."

"We're not together for real." I savored the first sip of my refreshing drink. "I asked him to be my dating tutor since I'm doing such a shitty job at it."

He snorted in amusement. "Oh, I see how it is. You're easing yourself into being with him by 'practicing' dating him. Clever."

"It's not like that!"

"Do yourself a favor and read North's *Real Fake*,"

he suggested. Since he was friendly with everyone in my social circle, he knew all about my friend North's career as a romance author. "It's an excellent example of faking a relationship until it becomes real."

"I'm not that lucky, though. Izzy's heart is an impenetrable fortress."

Red scoffed at my protests. "Uh-huh. Sure it is. It *totally* doesn't have a you-shaped hole in it that's his only weakness."

"If he wanted me, he would have already taken me." I tried not to feel bitter about it. "God knows I've shamelessly thrown myself at him for three years trying to tempt him."

"Did it ever occur to you that he has actual feelings for you that keep him from doing something when you always act like hooking up would only be for fun?"

I poked at the ice with my pink umbrella. "There's no way that's true."

"Maybe he keeps saying no because he doesn't want to be one of the many guys you fool around with. What if he wants to say yes to being the only person you love?"

"Okay, now you're making shit up," I said with a laugh. "If my best friend had those kinds of feelings for me, I'd definitely know."

"Would you?"

"Of course!"

Red gave me a skeptical look. "Then how else do

you explain that literally everyone who knows the two of you assumes you have feelings for each other?"

I waved his claim away. "That's because people assume our flirting is more than banter. It doesn't mean anything, though. I flirt with you all the time because it's fun, not because I'm secretly in love with you or anything."

"Fifty bucks says you two end up dating for real before this whole thing is over."

That would be an easy victory for me. "It's a bet."

Before we could continue our conversation, Izzy entered the restaurant. He always looked good, but he was extra fuckable in his dip-dyed white blazer with a fading gray gradient. It was cut to flatter his tall frame and paired with distressed skinny jeans. Anyone would have mistaken him for a model thanks to his impeccable fashion sense and gorgeous face. As he made his way over to where I was at the bar, he didn't seem to notice all the glances he was getting from the people he passed.

"*Bonsoir, mon ami.*" I stiffened when he greeted me with a gentle kiss on each of my cheeks. That close, I got a tantalizing whiff of his bitter peach, sandalwood, and patchouli cologne. It made me want to tug him down by the lapels for a real kiss and have him fuck me on the bar top while everyone watched. He distracted me to the point where I almost didn't notice Red's knowing snicker. "Were you waiting long?"

I shook my head because my voice wouldn't work

right as my best friend looked down at me with his honey-colored eyes that made heat pool in the pit of my stomach. What was wrong with me? It was just Izzy, so why was I acting so weird?

It was all Red's fault for giving me a ridiculous notion about Izzy liking me for real. There was no way that would ever be true. He was too smart to fall for me. I was the only one dumb enough to do that when I didn't stand a chance. Stupid, inconvenient feelings were the *worst*.

Taking pity on me, Red greeted my friend to buy me some time to compose myself. "Good evening, Izzy. Wren was filling me in on your new job as his dating coach. You've got your work cut out for you, don't you?"

Even though he was teasing, I had to protest. "Hey!"

Izzy chuckled. "It seems that way."

"Well, if you can help him, I'll gladly sign up to be your next student. My dating track record is depressingly abysmal. At the rate I'm going, it'll be me and Gonk for the rest of my life." That was the nickname of Red's cat, Algonquin.

For some reason, the thought of Izzy and Red on a date irritated me. "What about your no dating customers rule?"

His smug smirk was as annoying as it was sexy. "Uh-oh, somebody's jealous."

I crossed my arms over my chest and straightened up to my full height. "I'm *not* jealous."

"Really? Tell that to your face." His charming grin made it impossible to be mad at him.

"There's nothing wrong with my face."

Izzy reached out and caressed my jawline, sending electric bursts of white-hot heat through my system. "*Oui*, it's as perfect as the rest of you."

"Um, thanks." Why was I getting all tongue-tied and stupid? Instead of making my usual smart-ass comment about damn right I was perfect, I could barely get out any words. Why did my stupid feelings have to choose *now* to flare up and be all problematic?

He brushed my cheek with a fond look that turned me into a puddle. "Are you feeling well? Your cheeks are flushed. Plus, you're unusually demure."

"Yeah, I'm fine. We should grab a table." I picked up my drink to take with me and raised it in a toast to the bartender. "Thanks. I'll see you around, Red."

"Sounds great. Have fun 'practicing' tonight." The flirt winked at us for good measure.

When I got off the high barstool, Izzy reached out to steady me with a hand on my lower back. He then guided me to a booth on the other side of the restaurant. It was a small, intimate gesture that sent lust raging through me like a summer wildfire. I had to focus extra hard on not tripping over my own stupid feet and spilling my excellent drink on some poor bastard.

Once we sat down on opposite sides, I could breathe again without his touch clouding my senses. I didn't act that way on normal dates with other guys, so why was such a tiny thing affecting me so deeply? *Because it's Iz touching you*, the traitorous little shit who lived in the back of my skull whispered. I mentally gave him the middle finger and stuffed that jackass clown back in his box where he belonged. *Asshole.*

When Izzy looked at me, my brain did the worst magic trick in the world and forgot the entire English language and how to behave like a person. Things got worse when a tiny smile tugged at the corner of his lips as he tried not to show his amusement at my predicament.

I had a weird predilection for being attracted to certain parts of the body, and Izzy's lips were high up on my list of my favorite parts about him. They were made to suck dicks, and mine was growing harder by the second as I fixated on the thought. They were so full and plump; it was impossible not to think about them wrapped around my cock as he gave me the best blow job of my life.

Shaking my head to dislodge the inappropriate thoughts about my friend, I refocused my attention on not humiliating myself in front of him. Remembering I was supposed to treat him as a stranger, it killed all my normal topics of conversation I would normally talk with him about. It felt wrong not being myself with him, leaving me all out of sorts. I struggled to come up with something to say. "Uh, have you ever been here before?"

"Is that really the first thing you would say to your date after sitting down?" He arched an eyebrow at me that made my unruly dick twitch in the confines of my jeans. "When you ask that question, it sounds like you're the server who is about to explain how the restaurant works and what the daily specials are."

I laughed at that, which broke the weird headspace I had unwittingly fallen into. "Sorry, you're right." I rolled my shoulders with a subtle stretch and took a deep breath to relax. "I should've started by telling you how incredible you look tonight. Although, it makes me feel horribly underdressed in comparison."

"How can you say that when your shirt has a giant rhinestone skull with a mustache and diamonds for eyes?"

"Well, I had to get a little fancy. It's not every night I go out with somebody as hot as you." I had hooked up with plenty of good-looking men, but Izzy was on a totally different level from my dalliances. "I'm glad we're doing this."

"Same. I look forward to knowing you better."

I swallowed down my normal response about how much easier it would be to do that naked in bed together. If I was going to make progress with dating, I had to treat him as someone who wasn't my best friend who would laugh at me saying something so stupid and inappropriate. "I'm an open book. You're far more mysterious."

"What do you want to know?"

"Who you really are." It seemed like a good place to start, considering a lot of Izzy's background was a mystery to me. Even though we had been best friends for over three years, there was still so much about him I didn't know. He was entirely too gifted at distracting me from things he didn't want to talk about.

His lips turned up in an enigmatic smile. "Do you suspect me of being someone I'm not?"

"Part of me expects to find out you're secretly a prince living the life of a commoner." It was something all our friends joked about with him.

"Last time I checked, being the youngest son of a family running a successful vineyard didn't make me the prince of France. Even if it did, my older brother would be the dauphin, not me."

Arsène was as princely as Izzy and was living his fairy-tale happily ever after with our friend Felix. He had played tour guide for Felix on vacation last year and fallen stupid in love. It resulted in him moving from Paris to Sunnyside to be with his boyfriend. When I was striking out left and right, it was hard not to be a little envious of their romance that was worthy of being one of North's novels.

It gave me an opening to ask something I had always wondered about but never got around to bringing up before. "Arsène and Isidore are such unusual names. Do they mean anything in French?"

"Our mother is a big fan of Maurice Leblanc." He said that like I should know who the hell that was.

"Forgive my American ignorance, but the only M-name Leblanc I know is Matt LeBlanc from *Friends*."

He laughed at my answer, which set my nerves at ease. "Maurice Leblanc was a famous writer who wrote a very popular series in the early 1900s about Arsène Lupin, a gentleman thief."

"A gentleman thief? Does he say 'please' and 'thank you' when stealing stuff or something?" It was so amusing it took a second to process the rest of what Izzy had said. "Wait, your brother is named after a *thief?*"

"Lupin is more akin to Sherlock Holmes than a terrible criminal. He meets the infamous British detective in some stories, which Arthur Conan Doyle objected to. Leblanc got around the copyright issue by changing the character's name to Herlock Sholmes. Although, when a translation was published in English, it was switched to 'Holmlock Shears,' which is worse."

I laughed hard at the atrocious bastardization of Sherlock Holmes. "Are you joking? Because that sounds totally made up."

"It's so stupid that it can only be true."

"Okay, so that explains your brother. Where does Isidore come from?"

"In the third book, there's a high schooler who is a gifted amateur detective that gives Arsène hell. Our mother thought it a most appropriate name for a little brother."

The revelation delighted me to no end. "That's *amazing*! I'm going to have to read the series."

"I think you would enjoy them. There's also a Japanese anime adaptation called *Lupin III*. It follows the original Lupin's grandson, who is also a legendary thief."

"Oh, you know I'm watching that later." Anime was one of my great passions in life. I adored the *kawaii* hyper-cute aesthetic in particular. "Why is it every time I learn something about you, you somehow become more fascinating?"

Our server came over to take our orders and returned with white wine for Izzy. He held it up as he said, "Here's to a wonderful evening."

"It's already off to an awesome start." I clinked my glass against his in a toast. "Cheers."

"*Santé*."

It was hard talking to him like we weren't close friends. It meant most of our normal topics were off-limits, so I was scraping the bottom of the barrel. That thought gave me something to bring up with him. "Since your family owns a vineyard, you must know a lot about wine."

"*Oui*, I've picked up a few things over the years. However, I was more interested in my brother's work as a photographer, so I helped in his studio more than at my parents' business."

"With a face like yours, you should have been in front of his camera instead of helping behind the scenes."

He quirked an eyebrow, which never failed to be a turn-on. "What makes you assume I was only working behind the camera?"

My jaw dropped at the implication. "Are you saying what I think you're saying?"

"That depends on what you think I'm saying."

"Do you have a modeling career in France that I'm only now finding out about?" How could I possibly be discovering it now after three years of friendship?

His air of intrigue became more intriguing. "I don't know if I would call it a career per se, but I've worked for my brother as a model in the past under a pseudonym."

"Why use a pseudonym?"

"I preferred to keep that side of my life separate from my everyday one." He shrugged, like it wasn't a major revelation that he was a secret model on the side.

Since I had seen plenty of Arsène's sexy photographs, my imagination ran wild with the potential for sensual photo shoots. "What's your fake name?"

"If you're hoping to find out that I'm as famous as

Rune in France, you'll be disappointed." Rune Tourneau was the model from the infamous elevator sex commercial that I had come from more times than I could count. Our friend Callum had somehow been lucky enough to be engaged to him.

"Are you famous enough that your name will come up if I search it online?" I prayed he said yes, because that was literally the first thing I was doing after we got home. Knowing me, the second thing I'd do would be jerking off to it.

"*Oui.*"

Our server brought our food over, but I wasn't interested in my avocado veggie burger until I solved the mystery. "Do I have to beg you to tell me your model name? I bet your brother would tell me if I got Felix to help convince him."

Isidore sighed as he cut into his whiskey-glazed chicken. "There's no need to go to such troubles. If you search for Isidore Chevalier, you'll find enough to satisfy your curiosity."

I repeated the name to myself five times to ensure I wouldn't forget it before getting home. It was tempting to go to the bathroom and search now, but the wait would make it even better. "Is it exhausting living a secret life?"

He shook his head as he took a bite of his dinner. "*Non*, because it's not a secret."

"If it wasn't a secret, I would have already known about it." Tasting my veggie burger, I tried not to feel the sting of hurt over him keeping that from me. "Why wouldn't you tell me?"

"It never seemed important enough to mention, since I only work in Paris." He ate some of his mashed potatoes, distracting me as I watched him slide his fork out of his mouth as he savored the bite.

His point made me realize something else. "What about now that your brother has a photography studio here?"

"He's catching up on his long waiting list of American clients, so he doesn't need me." Izzy shrugged like it was nothing. "I only did it to pass time when school was out for the summer. Making enough money on the side that I wouldn't have to work while I was taking classes was a nice perk. However, I never had any intention of turning modeling into a full-time career."

"You could with how attractive you are." It was strange realizing if he was handsome normally, he must be even more gorgeous when photographed. I enjoyed a french fry as I continued pondering over the issue. "Why wouldn't you want to do that?"

He took a sip of his wine before answering. "It doesn't interest me as much as my studies do."

"I still can't believe you can study gifs at our school." It had blown my mind when he first told me what his major was. "Let alone in the *linguistics* department."

"My theory about gifs becoming an internet

lingua franca absolutely falls under the umbrella of linguistics," he insisted. "Certain ones have become a universal expression understood across cultures. It's a fascinating example of a common pidgin language that has replaced the need for words in some situations."

I loved it whenever Izzy flexed his intelligence. "You know you're the only one who looks at gifs as a lofty highbrow theoretical concept of abstract language, right? The rest of us are just laughing at dumb memes."

"I'm saving studying the evolution of memes as a nexus of cultural literacy for my master's program."

"It must be nice being so multitalented." Whenever he said smart stuff, my dick got hard. It made his air of superiority that much hotter. I shifted in my seat, palming my hard-on as I reminded it to settle down. There was too much dinner left to get excited so early. "What's it like being the best at everything?"

"You say that as if you're not gifted in your own right." He gave me the same chiding look he always did whenever I tried to put myself down. It was one of the few things I did he wouldn't tolerate. "You're a talented artist."

I had to stop myself from insisting he was better at everything than I ever would be. Sure, I could draw and was doing well with my digital arts major and Japanese culture minor, but Izzy was a different level of intelligence. Taking a deep breath to steady myself,

I tried to move things onto safer topics. "I'd love to hear more about you."

He was silent as he ate more of his dinner before answering. "I live with my roommate and best friend. He keeps my life lively."

I blamed the rush of blood to my dick for making me slow to understand why he was talking about me as if I wasn't there. How many times did I have to remind myself to act like we were strangers? It was so hard to do when he was the person I could most be my true self around. "That seems like a polite way of saying he's a pain in the ass."

"*Non*, my world is a much better and brighter place because he's in it."

Red's points from earlier replayed in my mind. I couldn't resist the temptation to play devil's advocate. "Really? That almost sounds romantic."

"Most of our friends assume it is." He pinned me under his gaze as he sipped his wine.

I drank several swallows of my blue lagoon drink as a flush crept over me, making it feel too hot. "Do you disagree?"

He chose his words carefully. "There are many ways of loving someone, some more romantic or platonic than others."

"Which is it with him?" I held my breath as I waited for him to respond.

His answer wasn't the least bit helpful. "I'm not sure."

"How does he feel about you dating?"

"I suspect he wouldn't like it very much."

He was damn right about that. The thought of him going out with Red made my blood boil, which was absurd when I liked both of them as friends. Things were getting too meta for my taste, but I kept playing the game out of morbid curiosity. "Does that mean we can't go out again?"

"*Non*, because he has not laid claim to me yet. I'd love to see you next week if you have time."

Thank god for autopilot, because my mouth said, "Great, it's a date," while my mind screamed, "What the fuck does *that* mean?" The coded double-talk gave me a headache as I tried to decipher his mixed meanings. Did he *want* me to claim him as my boyfriend? And what would that entail? Was I supposed to kick down his door and give him a hickey? Should I inform him he was my boyfriend for life because I claimed him like a shifter beast in heat in a romance novel? Was he giving me an invitation to fuck him and shoot my load on him, to mark him as mine like an animal claiming my territory? Did I *want* to do that? And god help me, what if he meant claim him like he wanted me to top him? The thought broke my brain.

My throbbing erection wanted him, but my head was a mess. As always, Izzy continued talking like he hadn't upended my world by floating the possibility that maybe he wanted me to make a move. If throwing myself at him every chance I got wasn't enough of an invitation for him to take advantage of, what else could I do?

I wasn't ready to admit to myself that I was *actually* in love with him and not just a little bit like I lied to myself about all the time. There was no way I was owning up to the embarrassing fact that I had fallen for him the moment I first laid eyes on him during freshman orientation week. No, that was a secret I'd take to my grave. I needed him as my best friend too much to lose him over me being stupid enough to catch feelings before we had even said hello.

Now what the fuck did I do?

Chapter Four

IZZY

FOR SOMEONE who prided himself on his impeccable self-restraint, I had fucked up during my dinner date with Wren. I couldn't bear hearing him put himself down, especially if it was to elevate me above him. My intention to praise him had somehow gotten twisted into a borderline confession disguised as a dare to claim me. I had expected him to demand an explanation, but he glossed over it as if I hadn't said anything out of the ordinary. Instead, he had grown quiet and pensive, which was the exact opposite of what I wanted.

I put up with it until we got back to the apartment. He tried to skulk past me into his room without saying a word, but I wasn't about to let him do that. I captured his thin wrist and pulled him toward me. "Wren, wait."

It was a good sign he didn't pull out of my grasp. "What?"

"Talk to me."

He avoided my gaze. "About what?"

"Whatever's bothering you." He tried to tug out of my hold, but I tightened my grip on him. "Tell me what's going through your mind right now."

He looked up at me with a guarded expression. "How much of tonight was true?"

"Even while role-playing, you know I would never lie to you."

"Sorry, but not telling me for over three years that you model in France is a lie of omission," he pointed out with a frown. "Did you think I'd treat you differently if I knew?"

That hadn't been the issue I thought he'd have. "*Non*, it had nothing to do with that or whether I trust you. It was unimportant to me, so I never mentioned it before."

"Then why bring it up tonight?"

I shrugged. "Because it came up in conversation."

He fidgeted in my hold but didn't free himself. "I don't like that you have this whole secret life when you know *everything* about me. Don't get me wrong. Your mysterious vibe has a sexy allure, but I hate being shut out of your life."

I used my grip on him to pull him into my embrace. "I'm sorry, *mon ami*. That was never my intention. You're still closer to me than anyone else has ever been before."

He wrapped his arms around me tight and snuggled against me like he belonged there. It was the best kind of heaven to hold him. "Sorry, don't mind me," he mumbled against my neck. "I'm all confuzzled."

I stroked his hair with a smile, loving when he made up words. That was his favorite way to describe fuzzy confusion. "Don't overthink it."

"Even if I overthink it, I don't think I'd understand what happened tonight."

"Then don't trouble yourself with trying to make meaning out of things best left alone," I said, hoping he took my advice. "Focus on the fact you did well and earned a second date."

That finally got him to lean back enough to look up at me. Everything in me whispered I should kiss him as a reward for behaving during dinner. However, I wasn't about to screw things up any more than I already had.

"It doesn't feel like a victory when you have to agree to it because you're my dating tutor." His pout did nothing to lessen my need to claim his lips as mine in a fierce battle of passion.

"That's not true. I could have declared you a hopeless case not worth helping." When he looked at me with horror, I gave him a reassuring smile. "We'll go out again when you're ready."

"Do you have any pointers from this evening you want to share to help me up my game?"

I urged him toward the living room. "Let's sit to discuss this further."

He blanched, even as he followed me to take a seat on our couch. "Damn, I must have really screwed up if we have to have a sit-down chat about it."

"You did fine."

"Yeah, if by fine you mean fucked-up, insecure, neurotic, and emotional," he grumbled as he curled up on himself and hugged his knees to his chest.

I held in a frustrated sigh. "Why must you be so hard on yourself? It was a wonderful evening."

He looked at me suspiciously. "Really? Because from where I was sitting, it was obvious I kept screwing up all night."

"No, you didn't. You put too much pressure on yourself to succeed. The best thing for you to do is to be your charming self. It feels wrong when you try to be someone you're not."

"But you told me I had to act like you were a stranger, which meant I couldn't be me."

I brushed a stray hair from his face in a gentle caress. "You should never date anyone who would force you to dull your sparkle. You being you is the true gift."

That finally drew a grin out of him. "Is that your way of saying you missed my nonstop attempts at making sexual passes at you?"

It was a relief to see Wren back to normal. "It's strange seeing you on your best behavior."

"Yeah, it's weird being so polite and proper around you." He laughed as he shifted into a less defensive position. "So, what's your professional assessment of why I never land a second date?"

"I suspect self-sabotage from overthinking everything on a first date. When you get in your head, you shut down. Not everyone knows how to deal with that."

He nodded in agreement. "That's fair. I do that kind of shit all the time."

"If you focus more on enjoying the moment rather than worrying about if it's going to lead to a second date or a bedroom, you'll have more success."

"Minus the part where I'm never successful in getting into your bed," he said with a pout. "At least with other guys, I have a shot—provided I don't fuck it up, of course."

"Of course." The words left a bitter taste in my mouth, because I hated the thought of him being with other men. There was nothing I wanted more than to get him into my bed and never let him go again.

His ornery grin made my heart skip a beat. "Is this the part where I ruin the moment by saying I'm going to go look you up now?"

My prick perked up at the idea of Wren looking up my modeling pictures and getting off on them. As tempting as it was to volunteer to give him a much more personal and up-close glimpse, I restrained myself to a smirk. "That would be a very you thing to do."

"Thanks for tonight." He caught me off guard when he kissed my cheek. "See you in the morning."

Before I could respond, he darted away and disappeared into his bedroom. I could only blink in confusion, at a loss for why Wren hadn't confronted me about my veiled references I'd made over dinner about him laying claim to me. Part of me had hoped that he would react to the dare by making a move. More than anything, I wished he'd give up on dating other men to be with only me. However, it seemed like I'd need to be more explicit to get what I wanted. *Merde.*

Using the bathroom before heading into my room, I dropped onto my bed with a heavy sigh. If I wasn't more careful, I would make a huge mess. The only thing worse than not being with Wren romantically would be losing him as a friend if a relationship between us didn't work out. It was one of the many issues that kept me from giving in to his flirtations. To be with him intimately and then lose him to another man would destroy me.

There wasn't a chance of him seeing photos of me online without getting off to them. It was both a blessing and a curse that he was terrible about smothering his reactions whenever he got off. The number of times I had pleasured myself while listening to him doing the same was downright shameful, but I rarely could resist the urge to join him. Hearing his breathy sounds of erotic enjoyment made my fantasies of being with him even more realistic.

I stripped out of my clothes and shut off my lights before getting back into bed. Surrounded by the darkness, I listened to the silence as I waited. Thankfully, Wren didn't disappoint me. The first giveaway was hearing him exclaim under his breath, "Are you fucking joking?" A few more seconds passed before he groaned. "Merciful Saint Fuck!" His whimper encouraged my cock to stand at full attention as I visualized him staring at my online portfolio with his mouth agape. If he was already invoking his patron saint Fuck in blasphemous prayers, it wouldn't take long before he gave in to his lust.

The sound of him undressing made me smirk as I took myself in hand. Starting with slow strokes, I imagined him getting more and more aroused with each picture he saw until he caved to temptation and jerked off. His strangled moan sent shivers through me as I picked up speed.

His office chair creaked as he shifted in the seat. It added another layer to my fantasy as I pictured him sitting in it with his legs spread wide. I was confident he was working his length with the same desperate need I was suffering from while listening to him. "Oh, *Izzy*! Iz, *please*!"

Hearing him calling out to me so beautifully, I

would have given him anything he asked for. It pushed me closer to release as my body arched up with pleasure. Usually, he only moaned and sighed wordlessly or with swears, so to hear my name falling from his lips was a rare treat. In my fantasy, I rewarded him by getting on my knees before him and sucking his dick. As his sounds grew more needy, I imagined him running his fingers through my hair and tightening his grip on me as he writhed under my attention.

He failed to muffle crying out my name when he came. It triggered my orgasm, my cum landing on my stomach as I pictured swallowing his release. His satisfied moan made me want to gather him up in my arms and cuddle him. Instead, I grabbed a tissue to wipe away the evidence that I was a shitty friend for getting off while eavesdropping on his private pleasure. Knowing he would think it was hot was a small consolation for something I knew others would rightfully find creepy.

With a sigh, I closed my eyes. I allowed myself to imagine how good it would feel to curl up around him and hold him as he fell asleep in my arms. Maybe if I got lucky, our second date would lead to that dream becoming a reality someday.

Chapter Five

WREN

WHEN I WOKE up the next morning, my first thought was about how sexy the photos I'd found yesterday of Izzy were. Jerking off to the memory of my favorites, I came all over my stomach and hand while softly calling out my best friend's name. It was probably fucked-up that I liked to be noisy, hoping he would hear me and get turned on by it. After all, was it my fault the idea of him touching himself while listening to me was hot as hell? I prayed to the highest powers of Holy Saint Fuck that Izzy would barge into my room someday and demand to fuck me instead of his right hand.

That was a fantasy for another time. Cleaning myself off with a tissue, I got out of bed to face the day. I put on my pink gingham pajama pants and a T-shirt with a print of a pineapple-shaped skull wearing red sunglasses. Leaving my bedroom, I pretended I hadn't just gotten off fantasizing about my best friend and roommate, who was currently cooking us breakfast.

Izzy made a turquoise ombre button-down shirt and black skinny jeans seem like high fashion. Now that I knew he had a background in modeling, it made more sense why he always looked like he'd stepped off a runway. He was too dressed up to be making almond oat banana crepes with hazelnut spread and a chocolate drizzle. And because he was so thoughtful, he already had cinnamon dolce coffee brewing for us.

I hugged Izzy from behind, but I was too short to put my chin on his shoulder. I had to settle for nuzzling against his back instead. "Breakfast smells *amazing*."

"*Bonjour, mon ami.*" He squeezed my arm in acknowledgement. "I thought it would be a nice treat."

"It definitely is." I sighed as I continued snuggling against him. If he wasn't going to reject me, I would take full advantage of it. "I'll enjoy pretending you're making this for me after a long night of wearing me out with carnal pleasure after our date."

Because he was so used to me being me, he chuckled at my statement. "Would that make it taste better?"

"Absolutely!" I reluctantly let go of him to make

coffee for both of us. He drank his black, while I loaded mine up with flavored creamer and sugar.

After he finished cooking, he plated the crepes like they were going to be in a magazine spread and brought them over to the table. They looked spectacular. Taking a seat across from me, Izzy gestured for me to help myself. "*Bon appétit.*"

"*Merci beaucoup,*" I said with a grin. He always laughed when I spoke French because my accent was apparently horrible. My first bite of the crepe made me moan with pleasure. It was so delicious that it should have been a dessert and not breakfast. "God, this is *incredible*. Living with you is spoiling me."

He tried his, looking thoughtful as he chewed it. "I wasn't sure about the hazelnut spread, but it was an excellent addition."

"It definitely was." I made a happy noise as I enjoyed another bite. "I didn't think it could be any better than it was last time, but you've outdone yourself."

"*Merci.*" It was cute how pleased he looked by the praise. "Did you sleep well?"

"As well as one can when they're alone."

He rolled his eyes at my blatant comment. "I guess I should consider myself lucky you haven't taken North up on his suggestion to 'sleepwalk' into my bed."

"If I thought I could get away with it, I would." That fantasy usually involved him taking advantage of my invasion by pinning me down and fucking me hard. "Since I have a one-track mind this morning—"

He arched a delicate eyebrow at me. "*Just* this morning?"

I wanted to make a face at him, but it was too difficult to do while I was laughing. "Fair enough. Anyway, when's our second practice date?"

"Isn't that up to you?"

I shook my head. "You asked me out, which means it's your call."

"Hmm, I suppose." He took a few bites as he pondered the issue. "Very well. Would you like to go out with me on Friday night for another date rehearsal?"

"Friday?" I pouted at the delay. "That's almost a week away. Why not tonight?"

"Because where I want to take you isn't open tonight."

It was a perfectly logical explanation, but I still felt salty about having to wait so long. "Where are we going?"

"It's a surprise."

I scowled at the answer. "Oh, is that how you want to play it?"

"Isn't it more fun for you that way?"

"I guess." Taking a break from eating, I sipped at my delicious coffee. "Are you at least going to give me a hint?"

"After yesterday, I'm confident you will *very* much

enjoy this." His alluring look gave away nothing but made me horny as hell.

Pulling myself out of the gutter, I tried to stay focused on the goal instead of thinking about what I did by myself after our fake date the night before. After wracking my brain, I couldn't come up with anything he might be referring to that we talked about during dinner yesterday. "How does it relate to last night?"

"You'll see."

He looked so smug that I wanted to make out with him. "Whenever you do things like this, it legit reminds me you're a sadist at heart—and probably in bed."

"You complain, but we both know you're into it."

I pretended to be uncertain. "Maybe I am, maybe I'm not. Why don't we get in bed and see where I stand on the matter?"

He laughed at my pathetic attempt to get him to fuck me. "Cute, but *non*."

"Hey, you can't blame a guy for trying." I shrugged as I continued eating. "Eventually, you'll give in to me."

"What would you do if I said *oui* to your overtures?"

"Uh, spontaneously combust my clothes and splay myself out on the nearest flat surface so you could take me?" We both laughed at my vivid description.

"Either that or die of shock that you finally agreed to make all my dreams come true."

"And in those dreams, do we ever do more than indulge your licentious desires?"

I could talk about fucking all day without being embarrassed, but his innocent question brought a blush to my cheeks. If he knew how much I wished I could cuddle with him, it would scare him away. It was one thing for him to turn down my overt passes at getting him to nail me; it was another thing entirely for him to shoot down what I secretly wished would come after the sex was over. *Blessed Holy Saint Fuck, please take away these stupid feelings I have for Izzy before they get me into the wrong kind of trouble.*

He continued looking at me with an expectant mix of curiosity. My window of time to answer without it coming off weird and suspicious as hell was rapidly closing. I had no choice but to go on the offensive. "Are you planning on doing something if I say yes?"

Izzy gave me a look that seemed to pierce right through my soul. It left me flushed and a bit on edge as his hazel gaze burned me with its intense heat. My heart raced as I stared back, holding my breath as I waited for him to respond.

His lips curved up in a slight smirk that made me think naughty thoughts. "I suppose we'll have to see how our second practice date goes."

I didn't know what to make of that answer, so I

ignored it in favor of keeping my peace of mind intact. If I thought there was even a remote chance Izzy would want to do more than fuck me, I'd lose my nerve to keep going on our fake dates.

EVERYTHING WAS normal between me and Izzy, but I still couldn't shake the layered meanings of his comments about me not laying claim to him. Not to mention him alluding to the fact he might be amenable to a relationship that involved more than meaningless fucking. I wanted that too much for it to ever happen for real. It felt like my soul had restless leg syndrome as I struggled to find meaning in his subtext.

After three days of getting nowhere on the subject and three nights of jerking off to his modeling pictures, I was feeling raw around the edges. I needed something to happen, but it seemed like he wouldn't make a move unless I did first. While I preferred the men in my life to take control, it was extra hard for me to show that kind of initiative. But if I didn't play the game, I couldn't win, right?

Getting up from my desk, I went out to the living room where Izzy was reading a book. His long legs stretched out on the coffee table, and he looked amazing in his baby blue sweater and dark jeans. He had always made it a point that he was available to talk if he was in our shared space. It meant I didn't have to feel bad for dropping down next to him on the couch. "So, I was thinking."

He gave me a wicked smirk that sent my blood rushing south. "About which position you want me to take you?"

It was so rare for Izzy to go from zero to one hundred like that, I almost didn't know how to answer him. It took a beat for me to recover enough to make a retort. "I've got a top ten list and nothing to do tonight if you're volunteering."

He chuckled as he set his book aside. "Perhaps another night. What did you actually want to talk to me about?"

"What date do you kiss someone?"

I cheered for my minor victory of his stunned expression. It was rare to catch him off guard like that. He quickly recovered because nothing ever stopped him for long. "Me personally or people in general?"

"You personally."

He shrugged. "It depends on the date. If I'm uncertain or don't want to scare someone off by coming on too strong, I might wait until the second or third date. *Pourquoi?*"

"What prevented you from kissing me after our first date?"

"You asked me to be your dating tutor," he reminded me. "I was only supposed to give you feedback about your performance on our practice date."

While reasonable, that wasn't the answer I was after. "But kissing is a part of dating." He didn't react to my point, so I tried a different angle of attack. "If I wasn't me, would you have kissed me if it had been an actual date?"

"Perhaps."

I refused to let him dodge my attempts at getting what I wanted. Upping the stakes, I straddled myself over his lap so he had to pay attention to me. "You can't give me proper feedback about how I performed on the date without knowing how I kiss."

"You've had plenty of practice with kissing," he said with a stern frown. "There's no reason for me to critique your abilities."

"But what if I'm terrible and that's why I can't get a second date?" I gave him my best puppy dog eyes. "I know you'd tell me the truth if I sucked at it."

He hesitated, but his arms encircled around me. "That's not a good idea."

"You're right. It's a *great* idea." I caressed his cheek, then rubbed my thumb over his full lower lip. It made me ache with lust to imagine my dick in his mouth. "I don't want to embarrass myself on our second date if you kiss me."

"I'm not going to kiss you."

"Come on, you know you want to. All you have to do is lean in like this." I demonstrated by cupping his face in my hands and moving closer. Stopping short of going through with it, I was determined to break his willpower. Of course, me being me, I got an inappropriate case of the giggles, which always happened to me at the worst possible time. "Sorry, sorry. I swear, I'm taking this seriously."

There was an exhilarating darkness in his eyes. "Do not play games with me, *mon ami*."

"But it's so much fun." I leaned closer at a different angle but once again stopped short of kissing him. "What if I dare you to kiss me?"

His voice was barely louder than a whisper as he warned, "Stop tempting me."

If he wanted me to stop tempting him, that meant I was getting closer to my goal of him giving in to me. "I'll stop tempting you when you give me what we both want." I was a breath away from our lips meeting. "Iz, please—"

He didn't give me a chance to finish my sentence. Instead, he tugged on my shirt to yank me down to claim my lips. I moaned against his mouth as he fucking *ravaged* me with passionate need. He held me in place by the back of my neck, teasing me with his tongue. I let him take everything from me he wished, melting against him as he explored my mouth and claimed me as his.

Izzy kissed me until I forgot what air was. All my thoughts fixated on how much I needed him to hold me down and fuck me until I begged for mercy. My pink sugar skulls pajama pants did a shitty job of hiding my raging hard-on trapped between us. However, I was too aroused to care—especially since I could feel his answering erection. I rutted against him as I ran my fingers through his dark hair, racing toward my peak at an alarmingly fast rate. The smart thing to do would've been to stop, go to my room, and get off in privacy behind the closed door.

Instead, I stayed right where I was and tempted fate. When he sucked on my lower lip before tugging on it with his teeth, it was all over. I came with a full-body shudder, whimpering his name as the best orgasm of my life crashed into me.

That finally caused us to pause our intense make-out session. We were breathless as we looked at each other and tried to process what just happened. My system was on overload, too overwhelmed to be embarrassed by the fact I had come in my pajamas like a horny teenager. It didn't help when he licked his lips to catch the last taste of me.

Izzy was the first to find his voice after clearing his throat. "Kissing does not appear to be your problem with getting a second date."

His attempt to sound professional caused me to laugh so hard, I had to rest my head on his shoulder as I lost my shit. The way he stroked my back sent shivers racing down my spine even as laughter made my body shake. "Good to know I passed Kissing 101 with my professor's stamp of approval."

"*Oui*, but you should see me after class about coming so early."

It simultaneously embarrassed me and reminded me about his dick, which was very much still hard as a diamond under me. "In my defense, that kiss was better than some sex I've had. *Wow*." I rocked against his hardness, earning me a slight hiss from him. "I'd be more than happy to make it up to you with a blow job."

"*Non*, that won't be necessary."

I gave it one last shot. "Because you're going to take me into your room and fuck me?"

It was inevitable when he dashed my hopes. "This game can't go that far."

I caressed the hair on the back of his neck as I built up the courage to ask a question I had been running from our entire friendship. "What if it wasn't a game?"

"That's a question best left unanswered." He tilted his head toward my room. "You should clean up."

"Are we not going to talk about what just happened?"

"There's nothing to say other than I shouldn't have let that happen." He gave me a not-so-subtle nudge to get off him. "Go."

It was hard not to take it personally. I slinked off in shame and returned to my bedroom to change. Part of me wanted to stay in there for the rest of my life and die of humiliation, but I wouldn't let that side of me win. Instead, I went back out to the living room and smirked when I discovered Izzy was in the bathroom.

He faltered when he came out and spotted me waiting on the couch. I derived immense satisfaction from seeing his flushed cheeks and lack of an erection. He could act unaffected all he wanted to, but his body couldn't fool me. It was so obvious he had finished jerking off to get some relief. But did it mean he wanted me for real? Or had it just been a long time since he had been with someone?

We sat in an awkward silence as we waited for each other to make the first move in the 4-D chess game that had shifted dramatically with our unleashed passion. I wanted to force Izzy to talk about his feelings. However, I wasn't in a place where I was stable enough to do the same without revealing things best left hidden. That meant the only other alternative was to play it off as a joke, just like I always did. "This is to be continued after our second date on Friday."

He frowned at my wording. "Second *practice* date."

"Whatever you call it, we're revisiting this issue afterward." Maybe by then, I'd have an explanation of what the fuck just happened and what I wanted to do about it. I couldn't resist a final parting shot. He stiffened when I leaned in to murmur in his ear, "If you play your cards right, I'll let you do more than kiss me next time."

He shied away from me. "You don't mean that."

"I've got a dirty pair of pajamas in my room that provide evidence to the contrary." I decided to go for broke and suck on his earlobe with a moan. "It's your move, Iz. Are you going to take your queen or not?"

Satisfied I had gotten the last word, I got up and went back to my bedroom for the night. My heart pounded from the thrill of being so bold. I had played my hand. Now, it was up to Izzy what he was going to do with me.

Holy Saint Fuck, please let Izzy make the right move and play to win for keeps.

Chapter Six

IZZY

NEEDING SOME PERSPECTIVE, I went to my older brother's house for some advice. Arsène opened the door and gathered me into a tight embrace. After spending so many years living apart in separate countries, I never took his hugs for granted. It was wonderful being within driving distance of him now that he had moved to Sunnyside to be with his boyfriend, Felix Murphy. The two of them had fallen in love after I asked my older brother to play tour guide for my friend. Despite their age gap, they were perfect for each other.

"It is wonderful to see you, Isidore." He gestured for me to follow him inside to his living room. "What troubles you?"

Taking a seat on his comfortable black leather couch, I gave him a look that told him exactly what was wrong.

A grin tugged at his lips. "What has Wren done to cause you problems this time?"

While we had lived in separate countries for the past three years, Arsène was very familiar with my best-friend situation. He always teased me about having feelings for my friend, which I of course denied. We both ignored that it was a massive lie. Sighing, I owned up to my current predicament. "I agreed to go along with one of his ideas."

"How bad is it this time?"

"I might have consented to becoming his dating tutor."

To his credit, Arsène stifled his laughter. "According to Felix, there is an entire genre of romance novels based on that scenario turning friends into couples."

"I'm well aware of that thanks to North teasing me about that while working on *Real Fake*." His book featured two friends pretending to date and falling in love in the process. *If only it were that easy.*

"What happened with Wren?"

I ran my fingers through my hair with a heavy sigh. "I tried to keep it platonic, but I'm doing a terrible job."

"That is a good thing, *non*?"

Shrugging, I didn't know what to think anymore. "It's making everything a mess. I'm playing with dangerous fire. I'll get burned if I'm not more careful."

"Perhaps letting the fires of passion overtake you and Wren would be the right thing to do, eh?"

That was what I truly wanted, but it wasn't meant to be. "He's doing all of this so he can be with someone else. The only one who's going to get hurt is me."

Arsène was sympathetic. "If you were honest with him about how you feel—"

"I *can't*." Dropping the pretense of protests I always used to protect myself, I spoke my mind. "He would never accept me being serious about him. It has to stay a game so I don't scare him off." I still couldn't shake the memory of him telling me to win the game by taking him for my own. It gave me a sense of false hope I couldn't afford to believe.

"You're not giving Wren enough credit," Felix said from behind me. He came around the corner and entered the living room. Dressed in jeans and a faded band T-shirt, his brunet hair stuck up in adorable spikes from being ruffled. "Sorry to eavesdrop on you, but it's true."

Given that Arsène had no secrets from Felix, it didn't bother me that my friend had joined our conversation. "He isn't interested in a serious relationship. They're too constrictive for him."

"Bullshit," Felix said with his trademark bluntness. "Everything in him is begging for you to tie him down and give him what he's too scared to ask for because he thinks he can never have it."

His description gave me vivid visions of me pinning a handcuffed Wren on my bed and fucking him hard. I shook my head to stop myself from getting too distracted by the tempting fantasy. "*Non*. If I tried to do that, he would run away."

Felix's smirk was wicked and beautiful. "Nope, we all know that he'd come all over himself while whimpering your name, then beg you for more."

His words made me remember Wren coming in his pajama pants from our heated kiss alone. I desperately wished I could accept that as evidence he wanted me, but it was probably just his normal horniness. "It's impossible."

"You really don't think you have it in you to hold him down and dominate the hell out of him like he's dying for you to do?" Felix scoffed at the ridiculous notion. "If you can't take charge of him, who can?"

"It's more complicated than that." I sighed as I tried to find the right way to express myself. "More than anything, I can't lose him as a friend."

"You run more of a risk of losing him by not letting him be your lover," my brother pointed out. "That kind of tension between you can only go on for so long."

"Trust me, the rip off your clothes as you give in to the inevitable part of the relationship is super awesome." Felix winked at Arsène, causing him to chuckle. "It's easy to do nothing because you're afraid of it going wrong. But it's worth it to defy your fears and embrace what you want. Wren will thank you for taking control of the situation. That boy is dying to be yours."

His logic was almost enough to sway me, but my reservations kept me from agreeing. "What makes you say that?"

Felix rolled his eyes at my ridiculous question. "Seriously? Are you *that* deep in denial that you can't tell how much he wants you to decide for him?"

My traitorous mind whispered that there was no difference between doing that and helping Wren by choosing dinner for him whenever he got overwhelmed. It felt great when he relied on me to take charge, knowing that he trusted me to always do what was best for him. There was no way it would be that easy about something as big as forming a romantic relationship, right?

When I stayed silent, my brother encouraged me. "Felix is correct. There is not a world where Wren would ever say no to being with you."

"But is there one where he *stays* with me?" I wasn't so sure.

"If you think he would stray from you once you gave him permission to love you, then you don't know him very well." Felix frowned at me with disapproval. "And honestly, it's shitty that you doubt him and his heart's desire to follow you to the end of the earth, whether it be as a friend or a boyfriend. He's been devoted to you since the day you met."

His point stirred up an uncomfortable guilt within me. "How can I believe that when he asked me to be his dating tutor to help him improve at seeing other men?"

Felix continued fighting for Wren. "Are you going to hold that against him when he assumes being with you isn't an option?"

"His idea is an attempt at trying to find out what you want in a partner, hoping maybe he can be that person someday," Arsène added. "Whether he is aware of that is another matter entirely."

When I said nothing, Felix tried switching tactics. "How long are you going to keep up this charade?"

"I need to end it after our practice session on Friday."

He shook his head. "I meant pretending you don't want him more than your next breath of air."

The truth in his words made my soul ache. "That's why I have to stop this game. I've already given in once. I can't make that same mistake again."

"What do you mean?"

I hesitated before admitting what had happened the previous night. "He approached me to ask if I could evaluate his kissing abilities to prepare for our second practice date."

"Wow, talk about a classic move from the fake-dating trope handbook." Felix cracked up into peals of laughter. "Let me guess: you gave in during a moment of weakness, had the best kiss of your life, and then forced him to leave to 'protect' you both?"

I looked away in embarrassment. "It was a mistake."

"Yeah, a mistake to stop," Felix corrected me. "Wow, I really underestimated your masochistic martyr streak. Poor Wren. He must be dying."

My brother gave me a concerned look. "I suspect they both are."

"It's not great," I admitted, causing Felix to laugh. "My resolve to resist is weakening."

"Excellent! It's about damn time." He flashed a roguish smile. "Bring Wren to Arsène's show on Friday night and blow his mind with the photographs of you. He'll be falling all over himself to be with you after seeing those."

"That was my plan."

Felix looked pleased by my comment. "Awesome, then you can put both of you out of your misery. Although you'll probably have to watch out for North while you're at the gallery opening. Even with him being with Elias, there's no way he's going to see you being *that* sexy without saying something about it."

I snorted in amusement. "I'm quite certain of it."

"In his defense, it's kind of brain-breaking to know that your brother took pictures of you looking like every gay man's wet dream. There's so many layers of what the fuck to those photos." He shook his head as we laughed. "We all knew you were attractive, but good god. Thank you for not walking around like that all the time. It'd give me a complex."

"I can only imagine the things you'd say if you weren't with Arsène. You'd be almost as bad as North."

"Yeah, the two of us would race to the lowest levels of the gutter if we weren't devoted to our boyfriends." Felix moved to sit on Arsène's lap, who indulged him with an embrace. "Now, our sense of decency will only let us get midway there, so Wren will take it all the way to the bottom."

I had to laugh at that. "Possibly."

"It will all work out," my brother promised me. He hugged Felix a little tighter, who happily snuggled against him. "It is your turn to be brave enough to be happy now."

I hoped he was right. Running away was only leading me to more problems, so maybe it was time to stop being scared and make my move. If it meant I could have the same happiness that my brother had found with Felix, it would be worth it.

Chapter Seven

WREN

WHEN IZZY BROUGHT us to the Sunnyside Museum of Art for the opening night of Arsène's photography exhibition, I felt like an idiot for not connecting the dots sooner. With all the confusion he had been stirring up inside me, I had forgotten about the event. It made more sense now why he had asked me to dress up my blue sugar skull mask T-shirt with a black jacket.

Izzy was spectacular as always, wearing a dark navy blazer that had beautiful silver filigree down the lapels. Nipped at the waist, it accentuated the graceful lines of his body. The white satin shirt under it only added to his princely allure. He looked ready to whisk me away to a royal ball and not just a gallery opening.

The first person we ran into was the last man I wanted to see. Armand Bellamy was Arsène's assistant, who was too handsome for his own good.

Not only was he tall, beautiful, sophisticated, and funny, but he was a notorious flirt who was far too interested in Izzy for my tastes. No matter how much he told me the man wasn't a threat, all my hackles rose whenever he set his sights on my best friend.

To add insult to injury, Armand looked like walking sex in a black-and-silver corset vest that had West Easton's hallmark touches of flair. It emphasized the lines of his lithe body and invited you to caress him all over and grope his perfect ass. Thankfully, he pissed me off before I had time to get horny.

"*Bonsoir, mon beau* Isidore," Armand purred in his sexy French accent as he approached us. He greeted Izzy with air-kisses on the cheek. "You look ravishing tonight. Wouldn't you agree, Wren?"

He absolutely did, but I refused to play Armand's game. Even though I was shorter than both men, I got between them to force some distance. "Don't you have someone else to harass?" I crossed my arms over my chest as I glared at the sexy bastard for good measure.

"Aww, are you feeling left out, *mon petit chaton*?" Armand reached out and pulled me into his embrace. The man was a walking pheromone who was a danger to society. That close, I could smell the blend of dark spices and leather notes in his cologne. It filled me with a weird need for him to tie me down and dominate the hell out of me. "I'd be more than happy to let you join us."

Before I could do something stupid like agree to a

threesome, Izzy pulled me back into his arms and away from temptation, warning Armand in French. I had to remind my cock not to get overexcited about the show of possessiveness when it didn't mean what I wanted it to.

Armand sighed in defeat. "You and your brother never let me have any fun."

"You're free to have fun without us." Izzy still didn't let go of me. That was fine by me because I wasn't in a hurry to leave. I'd stay there forever if he'd let me.

Felix came over to save us, looking gorgeous in a white-and-tan corset vest and jacket West also designed. There were few things she loved more than dressing the men in her life up in corsets. "Uh-oh, looks like Armand is making everything awkward again with offers for unwanted threesomes."

Armand gave a disdainful sniff, which was stupid sexy in a haughty way. "It's not my fault you're all a bunch of prudes."

"Oh, please. You're all talk." Felix gave him a knowing look. "Why else do you only proposition people who will never say yes?"

He wrapped his arm around Felix's shoulder as he stage-whispered to him, "*Shhh*, you'll blow my Cupid cover."

Felix looked up at him skeptically. "Your Cupid cover? What's that?"

"Hitting on the object of someone else's affection

is the best way to get them to act on their desires, *non?* It worked with you and Arsène."

"*That's* why you offered to have a threesome with us?"

Armand chuckled. "Either that, I'm an eternal optimist, or a shameless flirt."

"You forgot to add 'unrepentant pervert' on your list."

Arsène came over and pulled his boyfriend free. He looked stunning in his silver three-piece suit, paired with a royal purple tie and pocket square. "Armand, behave yourself."

"Someday, you'll appreciate my efforts."

He gave his best friend a warning look. "I would appreciate you leaving my beloved alone more."

Felix hugged his boyfriend and snuggled against him. "God, I love it when you get all protective. You're the sexiest caveman ever."

"Then my work here is done," Armand joked with a playful wink at Felix. "Perhaps I will go see if I can find Rune and—"

All of us simultaneously said, "Stay away from him." It was one thing for Armand to tease us, but it was quite another for him to upset Callum. He was the beautiful ray of pure sunshine in our friend group, who had to be protected at all costs.

He sighed in disappointment. "You must learn to tell when I'm teasing. It's a pity my sense of humor is wasted on all of you."

"You will have plenty of opportunities to find someone to entertain yourself with when you go to Hawaii next month to scout shooting locations for me," Arsène reminded him. "Perhaps that will stop you from causing trouble because you are bored."

North walked over hand-in-hand with his boyfriend, Elias. They were a textbook case of opposites attract, but their relationship was surprisingly sweet considering what an enormous pervert North was. Elias had opted for a dark gray three-piece suit with a black shirt and silver tie. North wore a flamboyant tan corset vest and matching leather suit jacket designed by his twin. "I'd ask how it's going, but it looks like Armand is in trouble again."

"What a rude assumption." He feigned outrage, but his blue eyes were bright with amusement.

"Between your normal trouble and all the surrounding temptation, there are plenty of things to stir up drama about." North pointed at me with a grin. "And based on how pissed Wren looks, I'm guessing you teased him about the hotter-than-sin photos of Izzy?"

I perked up at the mention of photographs of my best friend. If they were anything like the ones I saw online, I was in for a treat.

"*Non*, Wren is always mad at me. He's the only one who doesn't understand my considerable charms."

I rolled my eyes. "Your 'considerable charms' leave a lot to be desired, thanks."

Ever the peacekeeper, Elias did his part to shift the focus of the conversation. "This is an incredible gallery show, Arsène. Your photographs are truly amazing works of art."

"*Merci beaucoup*," he replied with a gracious tilt of his head. "I am pleased with how it turned out. Ah, here comes Rune and Callum."

Wearing a well-cut Gio Zapfirino black suit with silver trim and a matching vest, Rune's handsome elegance made everyone take notice of him. His sleek, sex at midnight, dark appeal was even more striking in contrast with his fiancé, Callum. He looked cute as ever in a stunning royal purple suit and vest with a pink bow tie as the perfect accenting touch. They were a beautiful pair of nerds who had found true love with each other when they least expected it. I was happy for them, even though it was weird when they first got together. Rune as a model had been a frequent fantasy in my spank bank thanks to his infamous elevator sex commercial. That had made for a few awkward moments for me while hanging out at their apartment.

I reminded my dick not to get too interested in watching Rune and Arsène exchange European air-kisses on each cheek. Since I was friends with both of their boyfriends, I pretended I hadn't jerked off to that hot fantasy one hundred and twelve times before.

Callum beamed up at Arsène after they also greeted each other the same way. "Oh, you've done such a grand job with the exhibition! And I'm not just saying that because Rune looks amazing in all your photos."

"Lucky for us, he looks amazing all the time, whether he's in a photograph or not." Armand pretended to pout. "Do I not get a hello?"

"*Bonsoir*, Armand." Rune gave me a new fantasy by exchanging air-kisses with my gorgeous enemy. "Still as flirtatious as ever, I see."

"You would agree it is part of my charming personality, *non*?"

"I don't know if I'd go *that* far," Rune said with a chuckle. "I trust you're still giving Arsène hell to entertain yourself?"

Armand grinned wolfishly. "I'd pretend to be offended if it weren't completely true."

"It's reassuring to know that you're as shameless as ever."

Felix grinned as he defended my enemy. "It's why he fits in with the rest of us who live in the gutter. Minus Callum and Elias, who are both saints for putting up with our nonsense."

Everyone laughed, because those two were the pure sweethearts of our group, who somehow were never tainted by our minds being wired for being filthy perverts all the time.

Before anyone could say anything else, West

came over and looped her arm through Armand's. She was North's twin sister, who was an absolute bombshell of a babe. Just like her brother, she had a wicked mouth on her that meant she was a riot to be around. She looked stunning in her black lace corset dress she had made herself and accessorized with a large chandelier-style necklace. "There's my sexy fashion model. Want to come flirt with my coworker who hasn't been able to take his eyes off you?"

Armand glanced in the direction she tipped her head in. There was a handsome man standing in a corner who was eyeing him like he was fresh meat at a market. The attention thrilled the playful Frenchman. "Lead the way, *ma belle*."

Once Armand left, I could breathe again. It allowed me to notice the photograph of Felix that was across from us. Entangled in the sheets, looking freshly fucked, and ready for more. It was a sensual side of my friend I wasn't used to seeing. "Wow, who knew you could be such a sex kitten, Felix?"

He blushed hard when he realized I was talking about the picture of him. "I'm not going to make it through tonight without wanting to die of embarrassment, am I?"

"What do you have to be embarrassed about?" Izzy asked. "It's a remarkable photograph."

Felix gestured around the room. "I don't belong in the same space as all these famous models. I mean, hello!" He pointed at Rune standing in front of him. "We're barely on the same planet."

"Nonsense. You are every bit as beautiful," Arsène told him, stopping his protest with a sweet kiss. "*Non*, I will hear no arguments to the contrary."

"He's right," Rune added, giving me a whole new fantasy to play with. I needed to quit imagining all my friends hooking up when they all had boyfriends. *Stupid overactive imagination.* "Don't put yourself down when you and your photo are stunning."

"Forgive me for not believing you when you look like you and there are photos here with gods like Rook Warrick."

The mention of one of my favorite celebrities got me even more excited about the exhibit. "Ooh, I need to go find his."

Felix blanched when he saw Augie and Brody coming over to us. He used Arsène as a shield to hide behind. "Okay, which one of you dicks told my brother about this exhibition?"

"Was it supposed to be a secret?" Rune asked in surprise.

"*Yes!*" Felix looked up at the ceiling like he wanted the earth to swallow him whole. "The last thing I want is my brother seeing pictures of me like *that!*"

"Too late," I said gleefully as they arrived. I lived for fun drama that didn't involve me.

His brother's boyfriend reached out and pulled Felix into a one-armed hug. Brody was a giant wall of muscle, who I had fantasized about pinning me down more than once. With his auburn hair, he looked incredible in his burgundy suit. He cajoled in his beautiful Irish accent, "Well, well, well. Our little Felix has grown up, hasn't he?"

He looked up at Brody with a pleading gaze. "If you ever cared about me at all, please kill me now." Brody chuckled as Augie gave his younger brother an expectant look. "Okay, before you get mad—"

"I'm not mad, but a *little* warning about what *kind* of picture of you would be here would have been nice." Always fashionably dressed, Augie looked amazing in his dark blue metallic suit with a red tie and pocket square.

"What was I supposed to say? 'FYI, I promised my boyfriend he could use a sexy photo of me in his exhibit since he gave me one for my book cover.' I already want to die of humiliation. Telling you that would have just killed me faster."

"Ach, you poor lad," Brody tutted sympathetically. "We all know I would have broken the tension by laughing my arse off at you."

"No, he would have given me a lecture about why I should never let anyone take sexy photos of me, even if I love them."

Brody laughed at that. "You've got me there."

Felix crossed his arms over his chest. "It's not like my dick's hanging out for everyone to see."

"It's art, Felix." Augie pulled his brother into a

hug. "You both should be proud of such an amazing photo."

Arsène reached out to ruffle Felix's hair. "I am."

Felix glanced over his shoulder at his picture, before grinning back at us. "I mean, I *am* hot in it."

"Try sexy as fuck," North said, causing everyone to laugh.

"There's my Felix!" North's mom Linda came over to join our group, giving him a bear hug. She was a vision in her powder blue tulle cocktail dress. She cupped his face in her hands. "Oh, would you look at you?"

He blushed again. "At this point, I'd appreciate if people *quit* looking at me."

"Well, try being a little less handsome, sweetheart," she teased him. "Arsène, you've outdone yourself. This exhibition is a marvelous tribute to your talents. Not to mention all your gorgeous models. And Rune, how do you seem to get even more beautiful in every picture?"

He brought Callum's hand up to his lips to place a kiss on it, bringing a blush to his fiancé's cheeks. "Because Callum makes me happier every day we're together."

"Not too bad for my favorite little storm cloud," a striking man said as he approached us. With blond hair, blue eyes, and a jovial smile, he was stunning in his royal blue three-piece suit with gold appliqué on the shoulders. The guy he was with was just as gorgeous in a dark emerald-colored suit, with delicate features, green-hazel eyes, and eyebrows that were so elegant, they rivaled Izzy's. My jaw dropped as the blond gave Rune a bear hug. Was that even allowed?

Callum lit up with excitement. "Jules, Xander, you made it!"

Rune pried the man off of him. "Everyone, this is my older brother, Jules, and his fiancé, Xander."

"Xander is also my boss," Callum added. "I'm so glad you both could come!"

"We'd never miss coming out to support my brother." Jules clasped Rune's shoulder and gave it a squeeze. "It's nice to see you again, Elias! It's been a while. How's it going?"

Elias smiled at him. "I've been doing well, thanks. I hope you are as well."

"Always!"

Linda chided Rune in a playful tone. "You have a brother this handsome and never brought him over to Sunday dinner?" Her weekly dinners were legendary amongst our friend group. "You've been holding out on me, sir."

He looked remorseful. "Sorry, I didn't want to impose."

She wagged her finger at him. "You know my policy is always the more the merrier."

"Just tell me when and where, because I'll never turn down a free dinner," Jules replied, causing his fiancé to shake his head. "Especially if there's dessert."

"Be careful what you wish for," North warned him. "My mom's notorious for adopting people."

Jules grinned at her. "Sounds great! I'll see you next Sunday?"

"You and your wonderful fiancé are both welcome." She really was the best.

Xander tilted his head in acknowledgement. "That's very kind of you to offer, thank you."

Brody gestured to a couple across the room. "Rhys and Lucien are here!"

As two more good-looking men walked over to us, Linda said what I was thinking. "Is *everyone* you know handsome?"

When they came over, Brody made introductions. "This is Rhys and his husband, Lucien. We were groomsmen at their wedding and best friends from college."

"A pleasure to meet you all." Rhys's chiseled cheekbones were to die for, and his gray-blue eyes were the kind you could get lost in. His light gray suit with pink tie brought out the color of them. "Xander, Callum, and Elias, it's good to see you, as always."

"We all work at Rhys's company," Elias explained to Linda.

"That's wonderful! Well, all of you are welcome to our Sunday dinners. I'd love to chat and get to know all of you."

Lucien had the whole nerd chic thing going for him with his glasses but was jacked at the same time. It was really doing it for me. "Thank you for the kind offer."

Izzy and I exchanged a few parting words before the group disbanded and went their separate ways so Arsène could continue mingling with his guests.

With no more distractions, the large gathering caused my anxiety to spike. I reached out to grab Izzy's arm and hold him close, because he was my steady rock in all situations. As he always did, he knew when I needed a break and steered me away from the throng to a less crowded section of the gallery. It made it a little easier to breathe. "Wow, there are way more people here than I expected. I always forget your brother is legit famous."

"It's easy to forget when he's so down-to-earth."

Absorbing his calmness, I looked at the surrounding pictures and was drawn to the one of Rune across from us. I had become so used to seeing him as Callum's doting fiancé, it was a shock to the system to see him in sexy model mode. He leaned back against a counter in a black suit, his purple shirt opened as he glanced at the camera. His icy blue gaze seemed to pierce right through me, sending shivers down my spine. I averted my eyes, because it felt wrong to get turned on by him in front of Izzy. "Same thing for Rune, too. How anyone who looks *that* fuckable can be such a huge history dork is beyond me."

The corner of Izzy's mouth curved up in a smirk. "Am I any different?"

I grinned at him. "Good point. You're way too attractive to always have your nose buried in your book, but that doesn't stop you."

"You are too much sometimes, *mon ami*."

The fondness in his eyes made my heart slam in my chest. Why couldn't he be in love with me? Clearing my throat, I tried to distract myself from my nervous flutters. "Why did you choose here for our second practice date?"

"I thought you would appreciate it."

I couldn't resist teasing him a little. "It's weird to bring me on a date to a place filled with enormous pictures of hot guys to lust over who aren't you, though."

"Then feel free to look at the ones of me."

I had gotten so distracted from everything that happened, I almost forgot there were photos of Izzy on display. He turned me around to face the wall behind us.

My jaw dropped at a picture of him wearing nothing but a pair of unzipped jeans he was pulling low on his hips with his hand. His other one held a necklace over his chest, drawing my attention to the sculpted muscles I had no idea his clothes were hiding. Izzy's unspoken "I'm going to fuck you until you beg for mercy" message came through loud and clear.

Biting back a whimper, my dick was hard as

diamonds from how badly my ass wanted that pounding his intense expression in the photograph promised me. Out of all the images I had seen online, that hadn't been one of them. It was sure to be my new favorite thing to jerk off to, though. I wondered if I could persuade Arsène to give me a copy?

"I have so many questions. All of them begin with 'what' and end with 'fuck,' so start talking." Tearing my gaze away from the photo was almost impossible, but I stared up at Izzy with shock. I could only make fractured sounds at him, all of my words broken by how hot my friend was. It took another four tries before I asked, "In the blessed name of Holy Saint Fuck, what the *actual* hell, Iz?"

He chuckled as he pretended to be innocent. "Is something wrong?"

"Yeah, there is. You look like that, but you're not fucking me," I hissed, feeling *very* put out by the slight. "And moreover, what kind of brother takes pictures like *that* of their sibling?"

"One who knows how to present every model in their best light," Arsène answered from behind me.

I subtly adjusted my raging hard-on before facing him. "Are you trying to break my brain?" I gestured at the image that was going to haunt my dreams. "There's got to be some rule about not depicting your younger brother as a sex god in photographs."

Izzy leaned closer to murmur in my ear, "That status isn't limited just to photos."

I elbowed him in annoyance, which only caused my suffering to grow as it made me painfully aware of his hard abs his fancy clothes were hiding. When had that happened? It had been a while since I had last seen him without a shirt on, but I didn't remember him having so much definition. They both laughed at my irritated huff. "Is there some reason both of you are torturing me tonight?"

Before Arsène could answer, a well-wisher drew him away. That left me glaring up at my entirely too amused best friend. "That picture is officially too much sexy for me to handle right now."

"If that's too much, then perhaps you shouldn't go into the other room."

There was no way I could resist that challenge. I grabbed Izzy's hand and headed to the next gallery. As soon as I entered, I stopped dead in my tracks at the sight of a photograph of Izzy and Rook Warrick. Locked in an embrace, they wore only blue jeans and smears of pastel paint on their bodies. They rested their foreheads and noses against each other in a beautifully intimate photo. Seeing my best friend and favorite actor together was the thing my fantasies were made of. My overactive imagination went one step further as I watched them kiss in my mind, with tender brushes of their lips that turned heated with passion. *Fuck, that was so hot.*

I wanted to be mad that Izzy had done such a sexy photo shoot with Rook and didn't tell me, but I was too aroused. With an epic effort, I looked away from the photograph to stare at my best friend. I had so many questions, ranging from "When the hell was this?" to "Where's the closest bathroom so you can fuck me until I scream your name?"

When I couldn't find the right words, I went with plan B instead. I used the lapels of Izzy's suit jacket and tugged him down to my level to kiss him hard. When he gasped in surprise, I slid my tongue into his mouth as I demanded from him what the photograph had inspired in my fantasies. I made out with him until I was in danger of coming in my pants again from the intensity of it. *I really need to work on that…*

Panting when we separated, I still didn't release my grip on him. I was done dancing around my feelings. "Home. *Now.*"

"But what about dinner?"

I moved my mouth as close to his ear as I could. "Sucking my dick will be your appetizer, fucking me will be your main course, and if you're a good boy, you can lick my cum off my stomach for dessert."

"*Nom de dieu*," he breathed in an awed tone.

Pulling back to stare up at him, my soul burned from the desire in his hazel eyes. "Is that a yes?"

"*Oui.*"

Chapter Eight

IZZY

I NEVER ANTICIPATED Wren to beat me at my own game. My tenuous grip on self-control shattered the moment he kissed me in the gallery. He made out with me like he wanted me to rip off all his clothes and fuck him against the wall while everyone watched. I was so aroused, I almost considered it.

As soon as we were back in the apartment, he was on me again. His demanding kisses and teasing touches kept my protests locked up in chains. I couldn't resist giving in to what I had spent three years denying myself.

Everything was moving in a blur, with our clothes coming off faster than I could comprehend as Wren stripped us both bare and guided me to my bed.

It was getting to the point of no return, and I had to stop us from careening off that cliff too soon. I put my hands on his shoulders and forced him back so I could think. "Wait."

"So help me god, if you say we can't do this, I'm going to lose my shit," he growled. I inhaled when he wrapped his hand around my prick and started working it. "I need this inside me, driving me wild. *Now.*"

As much as I ached to give in to my lust, I had to make sure he understood me. I guided him to sit on the bed, then knelt between his splayed legs. It was so tempting to take advantage of the position, but I couldn't do it in good faith. "I must say something first."

His pout was adorable. "Can't the talking part wait?"

"*Non.*"

He took a deep breath to steady himself. "Okay. I'm listening."

I was the type of person who preferred to rehearse conversations in my mind and plan out for every scenario ahead of time. Flying blind was not my style. But after all we had been through, I owed it to both of us to be honest. "You need to understand that this has nothing to do with being your dating tutor."

"And everything to do with wanting to jump my bones?"

"Oh, *mon ami.* You have no idea." I reached up and brushed the strands of pink hair that had fallen over his eyes to tuck behind his ear. "It's about so much more than that."

"Is this the part where you admit you've shot me down for three years because you thought I was only joking about wanting to be with you when all you wanted was to be with just me?" He couldn't quite smother his grin at my stunned expression. "Are you ready to confess your deep, undying love for me and me alone?"

My heart raced at the prospect of finally laying myself bare before him. "*Oui*."

I didn't expect him to double over with laughter. "Oh my god, are we really *that* dumb?"

"I don't understand."

Wiping away his tears of amusement, Wren had to take several deep breaths to calm himself. "Do you think I tripped into you accidentally the first time we met? I *literally* threw myself at you just to have an excuse to talk to you, because I had never seen anyone so beautiful in my life. Your sexy French accent was a *very* nice and unexpected bonus."

"You did an excellent job making it look like a real stumble." It was somehow surprising yet not at all shocking.

"The only part I wasn't joking about was saying I was your new best friend and future husband. I knew from the second I saw you that you were the one. But you only seemed to be interested in being friends, so I did what I had to while I waited for you to want me for real."

It was too much information to wrap my mind around when my prick was rock-hard. "But you flirt with everyone, so I thought you were only joking."

Wren cupped my face in his hands as he held my gaze with more seriousness than I had ever seen before. "Then let me be clear. It was love at first sight for me back then, and I'm still stupidly in love with you now. As smart as you are, how did you not realize all my dates and relationships go wrong because they're not you?"

I couldn't speak as I looked up at him, overwhelmed that he reciprocated my secret feelings.

He caressed my cheekbones with his thumbs. "I want to be your best friend, your boyfriend, your fiancé, your husband, your everything." He bent down and pressed the sweetest of kisses against my lips, before he pulled back with a cheeky grin. "And in case there was any doubt, I want you and only you to rail me into the mattress for the rest of my life. You have my word that your cock is the only one I'll ever suck from here on out."

I tackled Wren flat onto the bed and kissed him with all the pent-up feelings I had been holding back from him for years. My heart burst with the overwhelming joy of being on the same page as my best friend about what we wanted. I kissed my way down his body, caressing him all over as I claimed him for my own.

Getting on my knees in front of him, I spread his legs further apart as I obliged his years of begging me to suck his cock. His euphoric cries were a beautiful symphony to my ears. I loved how his thighs gripped me hard as I drank him to the base and swallowed around him. It didn't take much to make him gasp my name as he came in my mouth.

Swallowing his release, I pulled back to lick him clean.

Wren petted my hair with an appreciative moan. "Oh, that was *so* worth the three years of intense foreplay."

"And we haven't even got to the best part yet."

He scrambled to the center of the bed, stretching out on his back as he spread his legs and ran his fingers over his hole in invitation. "What are you waiting for?"

Now that I had permission to share my love with him, there was nothing in the world that was going to stop me from being with Wren. I paused long enough to grab lube before I worked him open with slicked fingers while kissing him all over. His needy noises fueled the raging wildfire of desire within me, making me burn for him in a way that made it difficult to take my time preparing him.

"Please, fuck me hard," he whimpered, squirming under me.

"There will be plenty of time for that later." I teased one of his nipples to a tight peak, then tugged on it to give him a hint of the roughness he craved. "I wish to worship you with my love tonight."

"If you *really* loved me, you'd fuck me so hard, I can't sit for days." I toyed with his other nipple with my teeth, earning a hiss. "*Yes*, just like that!"

"Tomorrow, I will give you the pounding you desire." I refused to rush after getting everything I wanted. "Let me show you a new type of pleasure this evening." I had every confidence that none of Wren's previous partners had ever made love to him like I was about to.

He continued pushing my buttons. "Not using a condom would be a first for me. Can we add that to the list of fun for tonight?"

The thought of being with Wren and nothing between us was almost too glorious to handle. "Are you sure that's what you desire?"

His grin was wicked and alluring. "Hell yeah. I want to feel you come inside me, then leak from my hole when you pull out."

I had to take a steadying breath, pushed to my limits with that kind of dirty talk.

He tightened his muscle around my fingers. "I'm begging you, please put your dick in me before I lose my mind."

"Ever the romantic," I teased him, but I obeyed

by withdrawing. Lubing my prick, I had to remind myself to stay calm as I moved to penetrate him.

I swore as his body spread to welcome me, sliding into his slick heat. Being embraced so intimately by him made me tremble with lust. I leaned down to kiss him with aching tenderness as I savored being one with the person my heart had loved for the last three years. It got even better when he wrapped his legs and arms around me to embrace me.

Taking my time building up to a satisfying rhythm, I caressed him all over as we rocked together. The euphoria of being with him was unlike anything I had ever experienced before, and I was in awe of how profound the moment was. I lost myself in the taste and feel of Wren, living for every soft sigh and cry I drew from him with each pump of my hips.

Cherishing him like I had never been allowed to do before, I fell more and more in love with him each time he called out my name. I flew to dizzying new heights, knowing that at long last, he was mine to adore with all my heart. More than that, I was his to love, which was the best feeling of all.

Chapter Nine

WREN

ALL OF MY sexual experiences were with hookups. I was used to fast and furious fucks as random dudes pounded my asshole like they were mad at me for something. That meant I wasn't a stranger to fumbling around with some guy who had drunk-dick before he passed out in a stupor.

What I *was* unaccustomed to was being worshiped by someone who made love to me with all of their heart. I hadn't expected Izzy to look at me with the utmost adoration, like I was the most precious thing in the entire world to him. The gentle pleasure of him showing me how he felt without words was unlike anything I had ever experienced before. It touched me all the way to the core of my soul as he showed me beyond a shadow of any doubt how much he adored me.

In the past, I had always fixated on having a

partner who wanted to fuck me whenever I was in the mood. I assumed that would involve me falling in love at some point, but I had never realized what it meant to *be* loved by somebody else until that moment.

Realizing that my best friend loved me with his everything was an overwhelming realization. I could feel the tears welling up in my eyes, because my heart was overflowing with too many emotions to contain them all. He exploded my soul into rainbows when he shushed my apologies and kissed away my tears as they fell. That kind of connection was everything I had never known I had been searching for my entire life.

There were so many things I wanted to say, which wasn't surprising since I usually talked the entire time I was fucking. But the profundity of the experience reduced me to only being able to moan Izzy's name as I clung to him.

My muscles tensed as I edged closer to the precipice of release, my body taut as a powerful wave of pleasure threatened to overtake me. All it took was him stroking my erection once while moaning "Wren" to send me right over the edge. My back bowed with the force of coming hard enough to see stars, the tension in my body disappearing as I became boneless in bliss. I almost cried again when he came inside me, deeply moved by him claiming me with the act.

With effort, I guided him down to kiss me so I could try to tell him without words how much it meant to me to be his. I had always fantasized about hot, demanding, passionate kisses with Izzy. But never once had I imagined what the tender brush of his lips pressed against mine would do to my heart.

Everything was a jumble inside me that was impossible to detangle with how incredible I felt. As always, he knew what I needed most, which was to say nothing at all for once.

I groaned when he pulled out of me, not ready for it to be over yet. He kissed my forehead as he said something to me I didn't understand before leaving, which meant one of us had forgotten English. As blissed-out as I was, it was probably me.

The moment alone left me hyperaware of his cum seeping out of me, which was intensely sexy. It made me feel dirty and debauched in the hottest way possible. When he returned with a warm washcloth, I almost wanted to tell him not to clean me off. However, I didn't resist as he tended to me. I was too busy trying not to cry again at how gently he was treating me as his most treasured person. After having run away from my feelings for three years, suddenly having everything I had been scared I could never have was a lot to process.

Izzy shut off the lights and got back into bed, pulling the comforter over us. He helped guide me to curl up against him, allowing me to use his shoulder for my pillow. It was tempting to drift off to sleep, but I knew I needed to say something—anything—to let him know how much our first time together meant. The only thing I could do was whisper his name in a plaintive tone.

He pressed a soft kiss against my forehead as he wrapped his arms around me in an embrace. "You don't need to say anything."

His comment seemed to kick-start my brain back into being me. "Afraid I'm going to ruin the moment?"

"*Non, mon cœur.*"

I slung my arm and leg over Izzy as I made myself even more comfortable. "What does '*mon cœur*' mean?"

"It means 'my heart,' which is what you are for me." He nuzzled against me with a contented sigh. "There is no need for words when I heard your soul's confession of feelings for me as our bodies moved as one."

"Wow, I'm not sure if I'm ready for you to be this romantic," I said, before I kissed his chest over his heart. "This is amazing. I never knew you had a secret schmoopy side."

"A what side?"

"Schmoopy," I repeated. "It's like schmaltzy, but cuter."

He chuckled as he caressed my bare shoulder. "When you define your made-up word with another fake word, it doesn't help me understand what you mean."

"Neither of the words are fake," I insisted. "They

both mean being excessively sentimental. You know, like being all lovey-dovey because you're head over heels in love with someone."

"Ah, then I am indeed 'schmoopy' for you."

It sounded a million times cuter when he said it with his French accent. "That's *adorable*."

"I think we can both agree that you're the adorable one."

"Can we blame me accidentally crying on that? Because that was super-duper embarrassing."

Izzy guided me to look up at him. "*Non*, there was nothing embarrassing about seeing your heart overflowing with such love."

"I'd prefer if my heart overflowing with love didn't leak out of my tear ducts next time." Even though I knew he would never hold that against me, it was weird to cry because a moment was too beautiful for me to handle.

He ran his thumb against my cheekbone. "Even if it happens again, I will always be here to kiss away your tears."

I blushed hard as I tried not to coo out loud over his declaration. "Wow, it's going to take some getting used to romantic boyfriend Izzy, because that was so sweet, I'm pretty sure you just gave me at least two cavities."

"For now, get some sleep." With a last kiss goodnight, he guided me to move so he could spoon behind me, making all my dreams come true.

I snuggled back against him with a happy noise, content on every level. Falling asleep in my best friend's arms was better than anything I had ever imagined.

WAKING up in Izzy's embrace was the best kind of heaven. I savored the moment, memorizing the perfection of his firm body cradling me close. Of course, since I was me, that meant my dick perked up from vivid ideas about how much I'd enjoy being pinned under Izzy as he plowed me. Since he was still asleep, I let my mind wander from one fantasy to the next. I enjoyed snippets of different scenarios, like waking him up with a blow job. Riding him hard and shooting my load on his perfect abs I couldn't wait to worship later was another satisfying one.

As I squirmed from too much mental stimulation, it didn't take long before Izzy's answering erection pressed against my ass. Desperate for some kind of relief, I whispered, "Are you awake?"

"Could anyone sleep through you moving so much?" He reached around and cupped his hand against my hard length. "Is this why you're awake?"

"That, and I'm hungry."

My predicament amused him. "And what would you like me to do about that, hmm?"

"Get us both off and then make us breakfast?"

He slowly worked my erection, which was sheer torture. "What do you want?"

His question left me torn between my horniness and wanting food. "A quick frot, your delicious vegetarian *croque madame*, then a proper pounding later?"

"That sounds like a perfect way to start a Saturday morning."

"Oh, thank god." I rolled over and shoved him onto his back, allowing me to straddle myself over him. Bending down to give him a good-morning kiss, I rubbed my erection against his in search of the exquisite friction that would get me off. "I promise I'll properly worship your amazing body later. Right now, I'm dying to blow my load all over your incredible abs."

He ran his hands up my thighs to reach back and give my ass a firm squeeze. "Whatever makes you happy, *mon cœur*."

I kissed him hard as I continued rutting against him like my life depended on it. He used his grip on my ass to help dictate the rhythm of my hips as I chased after my sexual high. I whined low in my throat with frustration, because while it was good, it wasn't enough.

Izzy reached between us, taking both of our cocks in his hand and stroking them together. I shouted as I thrust into his grip, which gave me a hint of what I was after. When he used his other hand to dip between my cheeks to tease my hole, I came with a full-body shudder. He climaxed with a soft groan, and I braced myself on trembling arms, admiring the sight of our mixed releases decorating his impressive stomach muscles.

Leaning forward, I kissed him before I trailed pecks down his neck and chest to work my way lower for a taste of us off his skin. It earned me an interesting rumble from Izzy, who ran his fingers through my hair with his clean hand in a gentle caress.

Best morning ever.

Chapter Ten

IZZY

AS WE FINISHED EATING our *croque madames* for breakfast, Wren's phone started going off with a flurry of rapid text message alerts back in my room. "It sounds like somebody wants you."

"The only person who wants me is sitting right across from me," he said with a flirty wink.

His phone continued making distracting noises. "Perhaps it would be best if you checked to see who is trying so hard to get your attention."

"Nah, it's probably just our group chat." He took another bite of his breakfast.

"If it was, mine would go off, too."

"Oh, good point." He wiped the corner of his mouth with a napkin before getting up. "If nothing else, I'll put it on Do Not Disturb."

He returned with his phone in his hand and a

furrow in his eyebrow as he sat down across from me once more. It left me with a pit of dread in my stomach. "What's wrong?"

Wren continued scrolling through the novel of text messages someone sent him with a scowl. "My friend Fox wants to set me up with one of his friends, Beau Chaton."

The news hit me hard, but the name was so ridiculous that I had to laugh. "Beau Chaton? That can't be anyone's actual name."

"Why?"

"Because it translates to 'beautiful kitten' in French," I explained.

Wren stared at me with wide eyes. "Wait, '*chaton*' means 'kitten' in French? What in the actual seven layers of bean dip hell?"

"What did you think it meant?"

"Armand always calls me '*mon petit chaton*,' so I thought it was some kind of French insult for a derivation of 'my little shit' because it sounds like 'shat upon.' Are you telling me this whole time, he's been calling me *my little kitten*?"

I had to hide my grin behind my hand as I smothered my laughter. "*Oui*, he calls you that because you are so cute."

"Oh, I'm going to fucking *kill* that asshole the next time I see him!"

The vehement swear drew a laugh from me

despite my best efforts. "Wait, so you're fine with him calling you 'my little shit,' but you draw the line at 'my little kitten' as being too much?"

"Yeah, because him insulting me since he's a jerk made sense, but *kitten*? That's too cutesy! And it sounds like a term of endearment, which is fucking weird when it's *him*."

"It *is* a term of endearment." I struggled to rein in my amusement. "Your protectiveness over me entertains him."

"I'm *so* going to knee him in the balls later," Wren grumbled with a scowl. "I'm not anyone's kitten."

I couldn't resist teasing him by reaching across the table to stroke under his chin like he was an indulgent pet. "You could be *mon petit chaton* if you'd like. I'll have fun making you purr."

He gave an impressive imitation of a growl. "Don't you dare make that sexy!"

It was too much fun riling him up. "Besides, weren't you the one who called Felix a sex kitten yesterday? Perhaps I should worry, eh?"

Wren huffed in annoyance. "Okay, in my defense, he totally was one in that picture at the gallery. But that's not the point! The issue is that Armand is—"

"Only joking because he thinks you like me," I interrupted. "He knew it pissed you off when he pretended to flirt with me, which made it more fun for him. I can promise you he is not and never has been interested in me."

Wren still looked suspicious. "What makes you so sure?"

"Armand has known me since the day my parents brought me home from the hospital when I was born. He's as much of a brother to me as Arsène. That's why he teases you so much. He sees it as his brotherly duty to help you understand you were jealous of him because you had feelings for me."

Wren ruffled his hair with a scowl. "I still don't trust him."

"It sounds strange, but teasing people is how he shows he likes you. The more he jokes with you, the more he cares about you."

He crossed his arms over his chest with an adorable pout. "In that case, he must be in love with me considering how much shit he gives me."

"You wouldn't be so mad at him if you knew how many times he's told me I should be with you. Believe me when I say he will be happy for us."

A small smile tugged at the corner of Wren's lips at that. "Does that mean he'll quit hitting on you?"

"Probably not, since your possessive reactions delight him."

"Well, I guess I can live with that," Wren declared. "After all, you're mine now, and it *would* be weird if he stopped being him."

His text alert went off again, reminding me of the unpleasant part of the conversation our detour had distracted me from. He shook his head as he read the message. "Seriously, who names their damn kid Beautiful Cat?"

"Someone who doesn't know French."

Wren laughed at that, which lessened the tightness in my chest at the thought of him going out with another man. "I guess I owe you an apology."

My stomach dropped at the implication of his words. "For what?"

He walked over and straddled himself over my lap. "I made you go through the hassle of being my dating tutor, but I'm never going on another date with anyone who isn't you."

I breathed a sigh of relief as I wrapped my arms around his waist to pull him closer. "Does that mean I owe you an apology for making it my goal to teach you how to love me?"

"Nope, it means you're an awesome teacher." He leaned forward and gave me a passionate kiss. "But if you want to fuck me hard and make me beg for forgiveness for being a dumbass for the last three years, I'm down for that."

"I could no more punish you for that than myself," I told him. "But if you wish for me to take you hard, I'm more than happy to give you what you crave."

"Don't get me wrong. Making love was *incredible*, but I really wanna fuck right now." His hardness pressing against me attested to that fact.

That was all I needed to hear. Sweeping him into my arms, I carried him back to my bedroom.

"Sweet Saint Fuck, it's so hot you can carry me like I'm nothing!" He moaned as he appreciatively kissed my neck.

Putting him down, I took off my black T-shirt and gray-and-purple flannel pants. Since he wanted it rough, I stripped Wren of his navy shirt and blue lattice skull pajamas. I wasted no time in pushing him facedown onto the bed, pinning him there by his neck as I slid my erection between his ass cheeks. "Is this what you want?"

He pressed back against me with a needy noise. "Fuck me senseless!"

I always loved a challenge. Reaching over to grab my bottle of lube, I pushed two slicked fingers inside of Wren. He may have wanted it rough, but I refused to hurt him. I prepared him under the guise of torturing him with slowness.

"Please, fuck me hard," he begged, grinding his arousal against my sheets for some relief. "I'm good to go, so *please*!"

Trusting him to know his limits, I withdrew my fingers and slicked my prick. I then lined myself up with his entrance and pushed inside him. He shocked me when he slammed back against me hard, taking me all the way in with a shout of pleasure.

After that, I gave him the rough fuck he had spent

the last three years begging me for. I held him down by the nape of his neck and fucked him as roughly as I dared to. It earned me the most beautiful of lusty cries as he kept pace with me. I was relentless as I drove my hips into him, teasing him with alternating short and long thrusts that had him shouting my name as he rocked against me.

When he tried to touch himself, I used my free hand to pin him to the bed. The shift in positions made him cry out, a wonderful noise I wanted him to make again. I took a chance and nipped at his ear. Tugging on it resulted in him begging me for more.

I could feel him tensing up, so I reached down and used his neck to jerk him up and flush with my body. He rutted against me, gasping with pleasure when I tightened my grip on his throat. I forced him to turn his head and kissed him hard, then shoved him back onto the bed.

Resuming my harsh rhythm, I leaned closer and murmured in his ear, "Do you want to come?"

"Yes!"

I tweaked one of his nipples to cause him to cry out again. Moving further south, I circled the base of his cock. "Do you want me to touch you here?"

"*Please!*" He was almost sobbing with need. "Fuck, I'm so close."

I wrapped my hand around his dick, then tightened my grip hard enough to make him groan. "You come when I say you do." I tugged on his earlobe for good measure, resulting in a shaky swear from him.

Since Wren wanted to be pushed to his limits, I did the one thing I knew would drive him to madness: I came before he did, then pulled out.

He groaned with frustration, pumping his hips to make me move my hand. "Iz, Izzy, fucking *please*!"

I shoved my fingers back inside him, brushing over the spot that made him shout as he shoved hard against me. "The sight of me dripping out of you is *très magnifique*." I withdrew from him, savoring the sight of my cum mixed with lube coming out of him as I did so. It made something inside me purr with satisfaction at seeing the evidence of how I had claimed him as mine.

Before he could say anything, I guided him to turn over. I bent down and swallowed his cock at the same time as I fingered him. One moan low in my throat and a single caress of his bundle of nerves was all that was necessary to make him shout my name as he climaxed.

Swallowing his release, I pulled back and positioned myself over him with a tut. "You came before I said you could."

"Sorry, too good." He whimpered, stretching under me as he luxuriated in the afterglow.

"I'll punish you for it later." I kissed him, enjoying his soft moan of pleasure as he tasted himself on my tongue. "First, I need to get you cleaned up."

He remained boneless as I forced my tired body to move so I could take care of him. As soon as I finished wiping him clean, I collapsed on the bed and pulled him on top of me for a cuddle. I needed nothing else as long as I had him.

Chapter Eleven

WREN

I FLOATED in a hazy day of sexual euphoria as I lay curled up on Izzy. Every molecule in my body sang with satisfaction at getting what I had spent three years begging for. It was even better than I had fantasized about, which was saying something.

My mind aimlessly wandered as I listened to the steady thrumming of Izzy's heart beating. But in true me fashion, I ruined the peaceful moment with a random case of the giggles over a strange idea.

Izzy continued petting my hair as he held me. "What's so funny?"

"Sorry, I'm having inappropriate thoughts about hearts."

Even though I couldn't see it, I could almost feel him arching one skeptical eyebrow at me. "What do you consider inappropriate?"

"Something cute and kinda morbid."

His chuckle sounded incredible from my position on his chest. "That describes the entirety of your wardrobe."

"True."

When I didn't say anything further, he prompted me. "If it's in line with that, then it's not so bad, eh?"

"It's weird and not at all what I should be thinking about right now."

He traced the shell of my ear, sending a shiver through me. "If it made you laugh, it can't be that terrible."

I hesitated before fessing up to the truth. "What if our hearts were prisons for our ghosts?"

He was silent before he burst into laughter. "*That's* what you were contemplating after we finished?"

"In my defense, I wasn't thinking anything other than how good I felt at first," I said. "But as I listened to your heart beating, I pictured a tiny ghost trapped inside, almost like in ghost jail or something. If that was the case, then what if your heartbeat was your ghost's chisel chipping away as he tried to break free? And when he gets his freedom, that's when you die, because your ghost leaves your body and isn't there to pump your heart anymore?"

Izzy rolled us over with another laugh, propping himself up so he could caress my cheek with a loving look. "As long as my ghost is trying to escape his prison in my heart, I'll never tire of your vivid imagination, *mon ami*. I'm sure he carves love letters to you into the walls with every heartbeat."

I grinned up at him. "Wow, I'm impressed that you took my creepy idea and somehow made it romantic as hell."

"Does this mean I should start calling you '*fantôme de mon cœur*' from now on? The ghost of my heart?"

I pretended to think it over. "You know, that's kinda badass. It makes it sound like I'm haunting you."

"Or perhaps I should start calling you '*mon petit tout*' instead." He brushed some stray hair from my eyes. "Because you're not just my heart, you're my little everything."

"Ooh, I like the sound of that." I reached up to guide him down for a sweet kiss. "Now, I need to come up with something cute to call you back. Maybe I'll start calling you '*j'adore*.'"

"Cute, but that's not an actual nickname in French."

"Yeah, but it's one of six words I can say in your language without fucking up," I retorted, causing him to laugh again. "And it's true that I adore you."

His smile was beautiful and filled my soul with butterflies made of sunshine. "Is it too soon for me to say *je t'aime* yet?"

If I got any happier, my inner ghost was going to break free of his heart prison sooner rather than later. "You're about three years overdue to say that, actually.

We have quite the backlog of 'I love you's to catch up on at this point. But what am I going to call you?"

"Normally, I'd say whatever you want, but I fear what you might do with *carte blanche* permission."

"That's fair. I'd end up calling you something obnoxious just because I could." I tapped my chin as I considered my options. "I could call you 'sin,' because you're sexy as sin and you make me want to sin all the time."

He grinned at my suggestion. "I'm sure your blessed Saint Fuck would forgive your wicked thoughts of what you wish I'd do to you in bed."

It tickled me whenever Izzy took my blasphemy seriously. "He always does. But 'sin' doesn't really work in everyday conversation. I'd never say, 'Sin, can you pass the mashed potatoes?' It sounds too weird."

"It's not ideal." He propped his head up on his hand as he made himself more comfortable. "I'm surprised you don't want to go a more gothic route."

"I could never call you 'raven' with a straight face." The mere idea of it made me laugh. "I could call you 'prince,' because you make all my dreams come true, plus I'm still not entirely convinced it's not your real title."

"Are you saying I'm your Prince Charming?"

I lifted my head to give him a sweet kiss. "You're the prince of my heart for sure. Oh, that would be fun!"

"You've lost me."

"I can have fun calling you the prince of different things." The more I thought about it, the more excited I got about the idea. "Right now, I'll call you Prince Darling. Later, you might be Prince Precious."

He chuckled. "Leave it to you to turn a nickname into a game of surprise."

"Isn't that why you love me, Prince Dearest?"

"*Oui*, now and forever, *mon petit tout*."

My heart exploded into an impressive technicolor pyrotechnics display when he leaned down to give me a tender kiss. I savored the moment before my brain kicked in again. "Oh, that reminds me!"

"About?"

"Something that has nothing to do with that." I gestured for him to roll onto his back, allowing me to straddle over him. "It's been bugging me, but I can't figure out how to ask you without it being weird."

He wrapped his arms around my waist in a loose embrace. "You can ask me about anything."

"In that case, I've got *loads* of questions."

"About Rook?"

If he was offering, I would gladly accept any information I could get on the subject. "Did you kiss him?"

"*Oui*."

Even though Izzy was officially my boyfriend now, that didn't mean fantasizing about a hot threesome with him and one of my favorite actors was off-limits. "Did you do more than kiss?"

"*Oui.*"

My mind provided me with very graphic and exciting possibilities for what that meant. "Did you fuck? Please tell me you fucked. I need you two to have fucked."

"We did, and more than once."

"Oh, you lucky bastard!" I was *so* getting off to that fantasy later. "Who topped?"

He smirked at me. "Who do you think?"

"It's sexy as hell imagining the two of you fighting for who's on top." I got turned on as I watched it play out in my mental movie theatre. "But you're both so dominant, I can't picture either of you bottoming. That's what my original question was."

My reaction seemed to surprise him. "If I would let you take the lead?"

"You mentioned during our first practice date that I hadn't 'claimed' you yet. I couldn't tell if you meant as a boyfriend or in a sexual sense."

He stroked my lower back to comfort me. "I was referring to as a boyfriend."

"Do you want me to take you?"

"You look like you want me to say '*non*' to your question."

Reminding myself that it was Izzy and I had no reason to be embarrassed, I forced myself to be truthful. "The thing is, I *really* enjoy being on the receiving end of pleasure. I have *zero* desire to be the penetrating partner. The two times I tried it sucked more than a factory of vacuum cleaners."

When he laughed, it loosened the tightness in my chest. "That bad, eh?"

"Oh, it was awful." I ran my fingers through my hair with a rueful shake of my head. "Nothing kills my hard-on faster than having to put it inside someone else's ass. But if you want me to—"

He shushed me. "I never want you to do anything you don't want to do. Except the dishes because I'm not your maid."

"Wow, thanks for giving me a fantasy of you dressed up in a French maid dress to enjoy later." I laughed at his exasperated sigh which his grin ruined. "Are you sure, though? I don't want you to be unhappy if that's something you want."

"This is why we're perfect for each other, *mon petit tout*. All you want is for me to be inside you, which is the same thing I desire."

It was too good to be true. "Really?"

"Can you imagine yourself dominating me without laughing?"

I dissolved into a giggle fit at the absurd mental image. "Okay, that's fair. The idea of me trying to top you is ridiculous."

"Should I ever feel the need to have anything inside me, you have plenty of toys we can play with to keep us both satisfied."

I leaned forward and gave him an appreciative

kiss. "God, you really are Prince Perfect. But what about Rook?"

"If you swear you won't tell a single soul, I won't keep any secrets from you. But I promised him discretion, because he's not out and doesn't want to be. I expect you to keep me from breaking my word."

Izzy's protectiveness over Rook made me love him even more. Holding up my hand, I swore an oath to him. "You have my word that I will only use the information for enhancing my private fantasies."

He chuckled before giving me all the juicy details. "Rook enjoys an aggressive chase, but he craves for a partner to dominate him more than anything else."

It was honestly shocking to hear. "Seriously? But he's *such* a top in his movies."

"Movies and real life are two separate things. He spends so much energy maintaining his image as a straight alpha leading male, it's exhausting. The thing he desires most is for someone to take that control away from him so he can submit and enjoy himself. However, he's not a pure submissive. What he enjoys the most is the battle to make him give in. He wants to fight you for it."

"Fuck, that sounds like you got nice and kinky with him." My imagination ran wild with possibilities. "If I was physically capable of arousal, I'd be as hard as a diamond right now."

"I'm quite confident you'll be getting yourself off on that fantasy soon," he said with a smirk.

I bit my lower lip as I looked down at him. "Is that weird?"

He laughed again. "It would be weirder if you didn't."

"Would it bother you if I jerk off to thoughts of how you had to fight Rook for top?"

His amused expression spoke volumes. "I cherish how vivid your imagination is. As long as I've known you, you've been very vocal about getting off to scenarios involving your favorite celebrities, characters, and friends hooking up, with you as both a participant and an observer. I understand that Rook challenging me to bend him to my will is too much temptation for you to resist. Fantasizing about that doesn't mean you don't love me."

"It just means I'm a pervert," I joked.

Izzy grinned at me. "*Oui*, which is why I'll never hold that against you. Getting off to your fantasies while we're in a relationship is no different than pleasuring yourself while watching porn. Saying you should only fantasize about us together now that we're dating would be tantamount to telling you to stop being you. I wouldn't do that when you being yourself is what I love about you the most."

With a happy sigh, I lay down on his chest and snuggled closer. "You really are the best thing that's ever happened to me. Thank you for understanding. And for contributing such a generous deposit of new material to my spank bank. It's going to be tough to decide which to indulge in first: watching you dominating Rook in a battle for top or you dressed as a French maid while polishing my knob."

Izzy kissed my forehead with a snicker. "*De rien.* Enjoy them with my blessing."

"I love you so damn much, Prince Sweetheart." Sprawled on him like a determined starfish, I basked in the amazing feeling of having a partner who accepted all of me. Even with my vivid imagination, I had never pictured what it would be like to date someone who was cool with me fantasizing about so many other people while understanding it had nothing to do with how I felt about them. It meant everything to me that he wasn't asking me to change or stop being who I was. That was why my all-time favorite fantasy would always be the one of us living together happily ever after for the rest of our lives.

Chapter Twelve

IZZY

AS SOON AS we reached the Hurly-burly Bar and Grille to meet our friends for dinner, Wren led us straight to the bar. While I preferred to wear a stylish teal blazer with white flowers decorating it and black pants, Wren kept it casual. He was adorable in jeans and a T-shirt with a comic book illustration of a cat grim reaper collecting skulls.

Red greeted us with a wave. "Hey, guys. How's dating practice going?"

"I have never been happier to lose fifty bucks before." Wren handed the bartender cash.

He accepted it with a laugh. "I'm glad to hear it. And I'm not just saying that because I'm fifty dollars richer now, thank you very much. I'm genuinely happy for you both." He pocketed the money and started making Wren's favorite drink.

I arched an eyebrow over the exchange. "Do I even want to know?"

Wren had the decency to look sheepish. "Um, he may have bet me that our dating practice would lead to us getting together for real."

"And you bet against us?" I made a tsking noise. "I'm so disappointed."

"Hey, in my defense, I didn't think I had a realistic shot at being your boyfriend."

Red passed him his blue lagoon drink with an amused snort. "You're literally the only person in the entire world who thought that. The rest of us knew this was the only logical outcome."

"I'm too happy to be pissed about it." Wren beamed up at me with all the joy that love offered.

"As am I." After Red gave me a glass of white wine, I held it up in toast to him. "Thanks for helping plant the idea in his mind that he actually stood a chance with me."

He grinned at me. "I may suck at dating, but I'm great at playing Cupid for other people. Just ask Elias and North."

As if summoned by name, our two friends appeared and came over to join us at the bar. Elias was in a well-cut pinstripe suit, while North wore a white button-down shirt with rainbow paint splashes on it. I never would have imagined that someone like North would happily settle down, but he was devoted to his boyfriend.

In true North fashion, he took one look at me and Wren and declared, "Oh, you two have *definitely* fucked."

It was hard not to laugh at how embarrassed Elias got by the crude proclamation.

Wren's blustery reaction said everything. "What—how could—there's no way you could tell that we—*if* we did."

He snickered. "Oh, I'm *so* right."

"Why would you say that?"

"Because it's true. And it's about damn time, too."

To my surprise, Red spoke in our defense as he handed North a pink drink in a martini glass. "Actually, you're wrong."

"There's no way! Izzy looks way too smug. They've totally hooked up with each other."

Wren crossed his arms over his chest. "He always looks that way."

"Of course I do," I said, feigning arrogance. "I'm French."

Red gave Elias a glass of white wine before he glanced around to make sure no one else would overhear him. "You're wrong because they didn't fuck—I'm pretty sure they made love."

North howled with laughter as Wren and Elias both hid their faces in their hands with groans. It was surprising to see Wren get embarrassed. Normally, he could talk about sex without a moment's hesitation. His shyness about intimacy was endearing.

After North reined in his reaction, he clasped my shoulder and squeezed it. "Way to go, guys. It's about time you two *finally* gave in to your feelings."

"But how could you tell?" Wren demanded. He self-consciously rubbed his neck as he glanced at me. "Did you give me a hickey or something?"

Elias replied before I had the chance to answer. "No, we all saw your passionate kiss in front of the photo of Izzy and Rook." He hid his smile by taking a sip of his wine.

"And the way you dragged Izzy out of there like a shifter in heat about to lay claim to his mate," North added. "It was a dead giveaway that you two were heading home to tear each other's clothes off."

Wren overcame his embarrassment to smirk about the situation. "Can you blame me?"

"Hell no, that picture was hot as fuck! And the one of Izzy pulling down his jeans?" North kissed his fingers like a chef pleased with an exquisitely prepared meal. "Beautiful. Nobody in their right mind would turn a chance at that down."

"Especially not someone who's been stupid in love with Izzy for over three years," Felix said as he walked over with Arsène. He wore ripped jeans and a white T-shirt, while my brother had opted for a gray blazer with a black-and-white striped tie and a button-down shirt. "Honestly, I'm amazed you're both here and not still in bed together."

My brother hugged me with a pat on the back. "We are all happy for you both."

"Oh, did they finally get together?" Callum asked hopefully as he came over with Rune. He looked dashing in his white suit with an aqua-colored vest and bow tie. Rune had gone with a sexy professor look in black-rimmed glasses, a gray blazer, navy vest, and plaid shirt with a tie.

Wren couldn't stop himself from smiling. "Yes, we're officially dating now."

"What grand news!" Callum's genuine delight for us was precious. He hugged Wren, then gave me one next. "I'm so excited for you both! We have to celebrate."

"Perhaps it would be best if we got a table," Rune suggested. As Wren and our friends made their way to the back of the restaurant, he stopped me. "I'm glad you're both free to love each other now."

I smiled at him. "It's nice not having to hold back my heart from him anymore."

To my surprise, Armand approached us, wearing a flashy black blazer with red-and-white striping. "Did your kiss at the gallery lead to true love?"

"*Oui*." I accepted a hug from him but wasn't the least bit surprised when Wren came over and forced us apart.

Despite my reassurances that Armand was not a threat, Wren still bristled at his appearance. "Who invited you?"

"I invited myself," he replied with a charming grin. "I had to know if the two of you became lovers after your kiss at Arsène's exhibition."

"We did, which means you," Wren said, poking Armand's chest for emphasis, "don't get to hit on him anymore. Especially now that I know you're like an older brother to him, because it's twice as creepy."

Armand laughed as he hugged Wren, who struggled in his embrace. "Ah, then my plan worked like a charm. I'm so happy for you, *mon petit chaton*."

Wren pulled back from him. "And you don't get to call me that, either. I'm *not* your little kitten."

"Oh, forgive me," he joked facetiously. "I'll start calling you '*mon petit chat*' now that you have blossomed into *mon beau* Isidore's lover."

"That's only marginally less insulting, you know."

Armand gave him an unrepentant grin. "But of course. That's why I must use it. Come, let's join the rest of your friends in celebrating this joyful day." He steered Wren toward where everyone was sitting as Rune and I followed them.

As we sat down, West appeared out of nowhere. She was beautiful in a cornflower-blue corset maxi dress with black lace trimming "Oh my god, is it true? Tell me you two *finally* got together!"

I glanced over at Felix, who gave me a sheepish shrug. "What? You know I had to tell her."

"Yes, and I'm very grateful that you did, Fifi." She

kissed him on the top of his head as she hugged him from behind. Their friendship was quite sweet.

"Now, you and Armand are the only single ones left," Wren told her.

She took a seat next to Felix. "I'm too busy having fun to settle down with Prince Charming. And we all know Armand will never stop being a playboy."

Armand always had to play the part of the contrarian. "Who knows? Perhaps I'll meet a gorgeous man in Hawaii who will tame me like Felix did with Arsène."

"God help whoever that poor man is, because he'll have no idea what he's getting into," Wren said with a laugh.

As we continued joking about what kind of man Armand might fall in love with, I reached over and squeezed Wren's hand. It made my heart sing to know that I had the love of my best friend.

AS SOON AS we returned to our apartment after dinner, Wren shoved me hard against the front door and ravished my mouth with a rough kiss. His hands fumbled with my button and zipper as he tried to tug my pants and briefs down.

"What are you doing?" I asked in between his searing-hot kisses.

He dropped to his knees and stared up at me with hunger. "I need to suck your dick, Prince Sexy."

My prick perked up at the sound of that, but I had to say, "You don't need to do anything."

He freed my burgeoning erection. "No, you don't understand. I *need* to suck your dick. I've been begging you for years, and now I'm allowed to do it, so please let me."

The realization that he meant he wanted to do it and not that he felt obligated removed any objections I had. "Are you sure you wouldn't rather do this in bed?"

He replied by teasing the head of my dick with his tongue, before sucking on it while looking up at me. He made a show of rolling my foreskin back, then drawing it back up, only to take more of me into his mouth.

I leaned back against the door as I adjusted my stance. "Ah, so this is what they mean by a cocktease."

"Wanna suck your dick so bad, Prince Baby," he groaned, mouthing the words against the underside of my arousal before kissing along my length.

"Then I'd suggest you do so." I ran my fingers through his pastel pink hair in an encouraging caress.

Holding my breath, I watched him take my prick into his wet heat. I savored the sight of his beautiful lips wrapped around me. He went halfway, before pulling back at an agonizingly slow rate. "Is there some reason you're torturing me?"

"I want to get you riled up to the point where you don't hold back." He started trailing kisses along my length again, then sucked on the tip. "I want you to use me for your pleasure without worrying about gagging me. More than anything, I'm dying for you to fuck my mouth without restraint. None of this stoic, stand there and passively accept what I give you bullshit. Got it?"

Nobody knew how to push my buttons more than him. My voice had a slight tremble in it as I breathed, "Understood."

"Good." His ornery smirk was the only warning I received before he drank me all the way to the base with a moan.

I gasped as he started working my length with bobs of his head at a quick pace. After the previous teasing, it came as a complete shock to my system. It was more aggressive than I expected, which was the best kind of surprise.

When he slowed down, my last few brain cells reminded me it was because he had made a very specific request. Tightening my grip on his hair, I forced myself deeper into his mouth. Wren opened wider, humming around my length as he continued working it. He gazed up at me like he was drunk on the ecstasy of finally being able to blow me.

While I normally tried to be contentious about not forcing my partner into taking more than they would give, that was what he had specifically asked for. It was for that reason alone why I allowed myself to thrust into his mouth, shallowly at first so as not to overwhelm him.

His reaction was to grab my ass and force me deep, which drew a cry from me as I hit the back of his throat. When he stared up at me with a challenging look and didn't gag, I got the message. I started with tentative thrusts but lost my sense of restraint as he gladly took everything I gave him. It was an incredible pleasure to fuck his mouth with abandon.

Unaccustomed to such a thing, it pushed me to my limits. I could feel the pressure building up inside me, my body tensing as I raced toward a fast finish. "Fuck, I'm so close!"

Wren did something wicked and new with his tongue that drew my orgasm from me with a shout as I thrust until I finished. He swallowed my release, wiping the corner of his lips with his thumb as he looked up at me with dark desires.

I moved to pin him to the floor on his back, ravaging his mouth to taste myself on him. His lips were swollen from the roughness, which was an incredible turn-on. I fumbled with his jeans to unfasten them, desperate to give him the same pleasure he had given me.

It surprised me when he stopped me. "I'll take care of this. You go grab the lube."

In my excitement, my brain needed a moment to translate. "Shouldn't we move to the bedroom?"

"Nope, I want to embrace my 'had to have you before I take one more step inside our apartment' fantasy and ride you right here. I'm out of lube packets, so we'll have to pretend this was a spontaneous decision."

I laughed as I gave him a quick kiss, before getting up to fetch supplies. Our night of fun was only beginning.

Chapter Thirteen

WREN

IZZY RETURNING naked and carrying a bottle of lube was a glorious sight. He wasted no time slicking his fingers and sliding them into me, which only made me love him more. "Is there anything else I should do to make your dreams come true?"

"Get hard again so I can ride you like I'm trying to win at a bucking bronco rally."

He snickered as he continued working me. "I didn't realize you had a yeehaw cowboy fantasy in your repertoire."

I laughed until I couldn't breathe and then laughed some more at his beautiful French accent making "yeehaw" sound dignified and cultured. Every time I almost got control, I'd remember the meme of the honeybee in Texas wearing a cowboy hat saying "beehaw" and lose my shit again.

"What amuses you?"

"You said 'yeehaw,' which reminded me of the 'beehaw' meme. Now, I can't stop imagining a bee in a beret with a wispy cartoon French mustache going, '*Oui*haw.' It's so absurd, I *can't*—" I gasped, cracking up all over again from saying it out loud.

He arched one of his perfect eyebrows at me. "Only you would have an erection, fingers inside of you, and be laughing about bees with mustaches wearing berets."

"Please, say it once for me," I pleaded. "I'm begging you, Prince Generous. Just give me one '*oui*haw' to laugh at for the rest of my life."

Because he was the best, he gave me what I wanted, even though it was silly. "Only you could make me chuckle at *oui*haw beret bees in the middle of sex."

It was a million times better hearing him say it. I had to wipe away the tears from my eyes from laughing so hard. "Oh my god, that's officially the funniest thing ever. I'm *so* making that meme later and sending it to our group chat."

"I'm sure it will be a hit among our friends." Izzy curled his fingers inside me and applied pressure to the spot that made me gasp. "Now that I have your attention, perhaps you'd like to move on?"

I propped myself up on my elbows to see that he was hard again. "Wait, already?"

He withdrew and put on a show of slicking his

erection with lube. "The sight of your uninhibited joy brings me a great deal of pleasure."

I tackled him to the floor and smothered him with appreciative kisses. "Oh my god, I really am the luckiest guy in the universe to have a sexy, moronsexual boyfriend."

"*Moronsexual?* What's that?"

"Someone who gets turned on by dumbasses like me laughing at stupid shit like bee memes in the middle of fucking." I moved into a better position over him.

He didn't take my joke the way I intended. "You're many things, but a moron isn't one of them. If you were unintelligent, I wouldn't be attracted to you. I love your mind *because* it's so unusual."

"Oh yeah, stroke my ego, Prince Hottie." I moaned, letting the tip of his cock slide into me.

"Wren."

The seriousness in his voice made me stop being an asshole about it. "Sorry, it was a bad joke. Thank you for loving and respecting me. Can I please ride you like a pogo stick now?"

His concern disappeared into laughter. "Whatever your heart desires, *mon petit tout.*"

I started a hard and fast rhythm, which refocused my attention on to sexier things. It felt great when Izzy reached back to grab my ass and help guide me, letting him hit deeper inside me. My arousal skyrocketed as I ran my hands over his sculpted muscles.

"Seriously, how do you have a body like this? I've never seen you work out once in the three years we've lived together. I've never heard you say the word 'gym' before."

"Not all of us believe that getting up before noon is a hardship."

The bastard looked infuriatingly smug about it. And by "infuriatingly smug," I meant "fucking sexy as hell." *Jerk*.

I traced the ridges of his abs, loving the feel of them moving under my fingertips as he thrust into me. "Hey, I've taken morning classes, thank you very much."

"At eleven."

I pouted at the implication. "That's still in the a.m."

"Says the man who slept through the class half the time, anyway."

"In my defense, attendance *was* optional since it was a lecture," I muttered. "The only reason I took it was because it was mandatory. And I still passed it."

He chuckled at my protests. "Only by the grace of your Saint Fuck and the professor taking pity on you."

"That doesn't explain your body magically looking like this." I gestured at his perfection as I kept going to town on him. "And PS: how dare you hide all this sexiness from me for three years under your fashionable clothes."

"I get up at six and go to the gym, then come back at eight to take a shower and eat breakfast."

It was a toss-up whether the information impressed or horrified me. "Who the fuck *voluntarily* gets up at *six in the goddamn morning* to go to the fucking *gym?*"

"Someone who enjoys working out alone in peace," he replied. "You know we have one in the building on the third floor, right?"

"Nope, that's news to me." I started to say something else, but a hard thrust up from him on my downward bounce made me forget everything. "Oh, fuck, I bet that means you could bench-press me if you wanted to."

He chuckled as he gripped my slender hips. "You are a wisp of a mite, *mon petit tout*. It is nothing to carry you to your bed when you fall asleep on the couch."

"Wait, so you carry me to bed?" I moaned at the image of him cradling me like a princess. "Fuck, that's so hot!"

He laughed incredulously. "Who did you think carried you there when you fell asleep in the living room?"

"I don't know. I thought I sleepwalked back to bed during the night." Knowing I hadn't been dreaming when I imagined him tucking me in made me keen with need. "God, you really are Prince Charming."

Taking my cock in hand, he made me gasp as I

scrambled for a hold on him. To my delight, he started jerking me off in a way that guaranteed I wouldn't be able to last much longer. My bounces became more erratic as I slammed down in search of the ultimate pleasure.

When he shifted his angle of penetration and rubbed his thumb over the crown of my dick, I came with a loud cry. I shot my load on his stomach in spurts as he pumped me until I finished. He then flipped me onto my back and guided me to hold my thighs as he fucking railed me until I wanted to scream from the intense pleasure. The sound of our bodies connecting turned me on even more as he fucked me hard enough that I almost forgot to breathe.

He held my hips as he pounded me like we were shooting our own personal porn video. It was the hot sex I had dreamed about for years, with him doubling me in half as he gave me the ultimate deep-dicking I had been dying for. My erection returned faster than I thought was possible as I sobbed for release from the intensity of the pleasure, my body moving to chase the high. But in true Prince Sadist form, he edged me like a pro, which only made me love him more.

Without warning, he slammed all the way to the hilt and came with a moan. Feeling his cum inside me drew my second orgasm, a gasp getting caught in my throat as my whole system went offline from the overload.

Izzy lowered my legs for me, then moved to give me a sweet kiss. It was a sharp contrast to the down and dirty fucking he had just given me. Then the damn show-off picked me up and carried me into our bathroom to clean me up. He truly was the best boyfriend in the entire world.

Chapter Fourteen

IZZY

PROPPED up on my pillows in bed, I was reading when Wren came into my room after his shower. He snuggled next to me and pulled the blankets over us. His closeness allowed me to notice a telltale whiff of peaches from him. "How many times do I have to tell you that you don't need to resort to using my bodywash for self-pleasure now that we're together?"

"I know, but I like smelling like you." He kissed my neck, sending shivers through me. "It makes me feel like I'm yours."

Setting my book aside, I wrapped my arms around him in a loose embrace. "You *are* mine."

"Maybe I was a cat in a past life."

I laughed at the complete non sequitur. "What makes you say that?"

"Because I want to rub you all over me to mark me as yours."

"Isn't it the cat who rubs on their human to make their owner smell like them?" I brushed my thumb against his upper arm as I held him. "I'm pretty sure that means you're supposed to rub on me to declare me as yours."

He nuzzled against my cheek like a cat brushing affectionately against its owner. "There. Now all the cats know you're mine."

"All the cats we don't own are *very* impressed."

He rested his head on my shoulder again, draping his leg over me. "We should get a cat. If we got a black one, I could dress it up as a kitty grim reaper, go viral, and live off the meme money."

"That's not how that works. However, I'm not opposed to having a cat with you once we live in an apartment that doesn't forbid them."

"If my therapist prescribes me an emotional support cat, they can't refuse to let me have it."

The idea of a psychiatrist writing a prescription for a cat and passing it to the patient made me laugh. "As amazing as that would be, there isn't a pharmacy in the world capable of filling such a prescription."

"Could you imagine how much better the world would be if it were a real thing? We need at least two kitties, though."

"Knowing you, two would quickly become three."

He pretended to sound offended. "Are you implying I'm extra?"

"Extra lovable." I kissed his forehead, making him giggle.

"Okay, Prince Smooth." He sighed happily. "Can I make a confession?"

It was too tempting to tease him. "Are you finally going to fess up to stealing my underwear?"

"Nope, that's definitely our ghost cat's handiwork."

"Our *ghost cat*?"

He pretended to chide me. "Jinx is going to be *very* offended you're pretending he doesn't exist."

"Ohhh, *that* Jinx," I said, amused by the joke. "Of course. How silly of me to forget."

"And for the record, he's not stealing your briefs. He's just borrowing them."

It took a serious effort not to laugh. "For what purpose?"

"I have it on good authority it's not for anything nefarious."

"Well, next time you speak to 'Jinx,' be sure to remind him it's almost laundry day, and I would appreciate having them returned so I can wash them." Knowing Wren, they'd need it. I could only imagine what perverse things he had done to them.

"Lucky for you, Jinx is very skilled at doing laundry and will make sure they're clean." He hurried to correct himself. "Not that they're dirty! He just wants to make sure there's, uh, no ghost cat hair on them before he returns them."

I ran my fingers through Wren's soft hair. "I can't decide whether the implication is hilarious or disgusting."

"Thank god you have the patience of a saint to put up with me." He added after a beat, "And our ghost cat, who also might have borrowed one of your shirts, too."

"Jinx is quite the petty thief, eh?"

Wren shrugged. "Maybe he enjoys wearing it because it smells like you and makes him feel like you're hugging him when you're not around."

It was too much cuteness for my heart to take. "In that case, he's welcome to keep it a little longer."

He cooed with happiness. "You're so good to me. Um, I mean *us*."

With that resolved, I reminded him of his original intention. "I believe you were supposed to be confessing something else to me, *non*?"

"The good news is, it's way less embarrassing than Jinx's hijinks."

I braced myself for what could come next. "Okay."

He took a deep breath before speaking. "This is everything I wanted but thought I could never have."

I didn't quite follow. "What is?"

"This. Snuggling in bed with you, joking around, just *being* with each other without needing to fuck every minute of the day." He wrapped his arm around me to give me a hug. "I was so scared to let myself want this. If I did, it would mean I was really in love with you instead of just a tiny bit like I lied to myself I was. Getting shot down when I made passes was one thing. Having you turn down what I wanted most in the world would have been more heartbreak than I could've handled."

His confession moved my heart and made me hug him tighter. "Ah, *mon petit tout*, if you only knew. This was everything I've ever wanted, which was *why* I had to refuse your sexual advances before. Having the pleasure of you physically but not being allowed to have this quiet joy for the rest of my life kept me from giving in to you."

"I still feel like I owe you an apology for being so dense."

"*Non*, there is no need for such things," I told him. "Both of us were so busy protecting our hearts, we were too scared to take the chance until we were ready. There's no one to blame here."

He was silent for a time, stroking the nape of my neck as he sorted through his thoughts. He finally said, "It's going to sound weird, but realizing sometimes I *don't* want to fuck you is how I realized I loved you. Out of all the things I've fantasized about with people, you're the only one I've ever pictured myself having this kind of life with."

I tilted his head to allow us to make eye contact. "And what a life it will be." I gave him a sweet kiss, lingering in the tender moment.

His jubilant smile was beautiful. "I'm looking forward to it, Prince Forever."

"As am I, *mon petit tout*."

He curled up at my side again as he held me. "Read to me?"

"Anything for you." Picking up my book once more, I began reading out loud in French to Wren as I hugged him with my other arm. There was no greater happiness than having him by my side, embracing me with all the love in his heart.

Chapter Fifteen

WREN

IZZY PUT up with me being antsy until the end of breakfast before he tried to get to the bottom of my issue. "What's wrong?"

"Nothing." I fidgeted as I continued to feel foolish. "I'm just regretting not asking you something earlier when I had the chance."

He quirked an eyebrow upward. "And what's stopping you from asking me now?"

"You're not my dating tutor anymore."

He couldn't hide his grin at my predicament. "What kind of question can you ask your dating coach that you can't ask your boyfriend?"

"You're going to laugh."

"Probably."

I pouted at his answer, even though I was howling with laughter on the inside. "It's stupid."

"Let me be the judge of that." He gestured for me to continue.

Taking a deep breath, I forged ahead. "How do you ask your boyfriend out on a date?" As I predicted, he doubled over from laughter. "Hey! It's a legit question when I've never had a serious boyfriend before."

"*Pardon.*" He did his best to recover his composure. "Ask me like you would normally when suggesting we do something."

I frowned at his advice. "But is it really asking you out on a date if all I ask is, 'Wanna get dinner tonight?' That's how I'd do it when I was only your friend."

"You're *très* adorable. There's no need for things to be more formal because we're a couple. If you want to go somewhere or do something with me, all you have to do is ask."

"In that case, do you want to do dinner tonight? We've been on practice dates, but I want to go on a real one with you."

The fond look he gave me melted me into a puddle of goo. "*Oui*, I would enjoy that very much."

"So, do I have to meet you there separately because it's a date? Or can we go together?"

He reached across the kitchen table to take my hand. "*Mon petit tout*, there are no rules about what makes something 'officially' a date. We live together, so we can go together. You're overthinking this when there's no need."

I squeezed his hand in appreciation. "But I don't want to screw things up by blurring the line between hanging out like we always do and a date. I mean, what makes going out on a date as a couple different from us as friends going to a movie or getting dinner together like normal?"

"Coming home and making love to you." He raised my hand to his lips to press a kiss on the back of it, sending my heart aflutter. "We don't need a candlelight dinner and a bed of roses to call something an 'official' date. There's nothing wrong with us going somewhere normal and acting the way we always have. It's special because we're spending time together, not because we're doing something fancy. All I ever want is for you to be yourself and have fun."

"Are you saying it would still be a date if we ate at *Bueno, Bonito, y Barato* tonight and just hung out like we normally do?" I really hoped he said yes since I was craving their cheese enchiladas something fierce. It was a no-frills Mexican restaurant that lived up to their name of *Good, Beautiful, and Cheap*.

"*Oui.*"

I got up and walked over to sit in his lap. Looping my arms over his neck, I gave him a sweet kiss. "You really are too perfect to be true."

He embraced me back. "The only difference between what we used to do before being boyfriends and now is I'm allowed to love you. We don't have to act, dress, or do anything differently than before, because that's the you I fell for, with your skulls, hearts, and all your quirks."

I gave him another kiss, my heart overflowing with joy as I basked in the awesomeness of being in love with my best friend. "In that case, it's a date, Prince Awesome."

WITH THE PRESSURE taken off me, I was free to enjoy our first actual date. Taking Izzy at his word, I wore jeans and a black T-shirt with a tattoo-style sugar skull with flowers that said, "I'm my own kind of beautiful." Since he was always Monsieur Stylish, he looked amazing in a turquoise-and-black floral blazer with a white shirt and black skinny jeans that made his ass look incredible.

As we enjoyed the chips and salsa, I couldn't resist testing his theory that acting normally still qualified as a date. "What's your fantasy?"

"For what?"

"For me." I ate a chip as he continued looking puzzled. "What you'd like to do to me."

It was hard to tell if he was deliberately being obtuse or genuinely confused. Sometimes it was difficult to judge with him. "Right now?"

"No, sexually in general." When he had no reaction, I kept trying harder. "I have a million of them about you. The one of you in the French maid costume is getting a lot of playtime in my brain lately, not gonna lie. Your long legs, that short skirt, and stiletto heels? Fuck yeah, Prince Temptation."

He shook his head as I got lost in my mental movie theatre that always had a film of him ready to go.

Getting myself back on track, I continued trying to get info out of him. "Like, what *do* you think about when you're pleasuring yourself?" That thought alone was something I had gotten off to before on numerous occasions.

He grinned roguishly at my question. "Are you asking if you star in all my fantasies?"

"I don't need to star in all of them. I just want to know what I do that really gets you going?"

He took a sip of his margarita before answering. "You're you."

I made a face at his answer. "That's not specific enough. I want details."

"In my dreams, you're always being yourself. You're naked and kick open my bedroom door to demand I fuck you. You tease me while we're on the couch until I can't take it anymore and I have to have you. Sometimes, I turn around while making breakfast and you're naked and aroused on the kitchen table, saying something silly like you're sunny side up and it's time to flip you over."

I laughed until I coughed from almost choking. "Oh my god, that's *hilarious*! I'm mad I never thought of that one myself. Your fantasy me is a genius."

He challenged me, which was hot as hell. "Is that or is that not something you would do?"

"Oh, that's something I'm *going* to do, Prince Clever." There was no way in hell I would pass up a chance to make that dream come true. "Tell me more."

"When I go to do laundry, you're wearing one of my button-down shirts. You tell me if I want to wash it, I'll have to strip you first."

I snickered at how very me that sounded. "Let's be honest. It's a miracle that hasn't happened yet. Keep going."

"You sneak into the shower with me and tell me you're so dirty, I need to help you get clean. You get bored during a movie and give me a blow job to entertain yourself. I walk in on you getting off to my modeling pictures, so you beg me to fuck you. As I pleasure myself while listening to you jerking off in your room, you come in and catch me, so we get off together."

I mentally took notes, because all the scenarios sounded like things we needed to make happen for real. "What's one of your favorites that you revisit all the time?"

There was a slight flush in his cheeks as he confessed. "You ask me if I'll help you study for your fuckology class by practicing different positions with you."

I cracked up so hard, the people at the table across from us shot me a dirty look, but I didn't care. "*Fuckology*? What the hell is that?"

"The class you take to become a fuckologist, which is someone who studies fucking." He said it like it was the most logical, self-explanatory answer in the world.

"Oh, *please* sign me up for that major so I can have a new career. Holy shit, I'm a galaxy-brained genius in your fantasies."

"Like I said, the thing I enjoy most is you being you." He shrugged as he took another drink. "There's never a dull moment with you, whether it's the real you or the you in my mind."

The more I thought about it, the more impressed I was by his spank bank versions of me. "Wow, you actually love me for me, don't you?"

"Did you doubt that?"

"No, but all of those legitimately sound like things I would do," I said in awe. "You really know me better than anyone. I'm a little shit even in your wildest dreams, because me being batshit bonkers is what you enjoy the most, isn't it?"

He grinned at my description. "My life was very boring until I met you. You bring all the color and joy into my world by being unabashedly yourself."

"One, that's wildly romantic and I love you for it.

Two, we're going to make all your dreams come true later, Prince Lucky."

"*Trop bien.*"

"Okay, last question on the subject before we can move on." I leaned forward with a grin. "Do you fantasize about teaching me French? Because I've enjoyed that scenario more times than I can count."

He chuckled before taking a drink. "*Oui*, and you often deliberately mispronounce things to get me to punish you in the sexiest ways possible."

I couldn't stop laughing, because it was the exact same thing I had gotten myself off to so many times in the past. He really was my best friend, who knew everything that made me tick but somehow loved me for it, anyway. I didn't know why I was so lucky, but I was so damn grateful for being so blessed.

Thanks for coming through for me, Saint Fuck.

Chapter Sixteen

IZZY

AFTER COMING HOME from our date at the Mexican restaurant, Wren excused himself to use the bathroom. It gave me enough time to ready my surprise for him. I had been looking forward to it since I rarely had the chance to catch him off guard.

Between his previous mentions of me dressed as a maid and knowing how much he loved anime, my idea was sure to be a hit. The Japanese cosplay maid dress was much cuter than the stereotypical French outfit, with large black bell sleeves, a faux corset, and a white lace collar. To give it the full effect, I put on a pink ombre pigtails wig, fishnet stockings attached to black lace garter belts, and patent leather stiletto heels. I checked in my mirror, satisfied that I was the picture of demure femininity with a hint of kink to make him lose his mind.

Wren's reaction when he entered my room was

priceless. He stopped dead in his tracks, staring at me with his mouth open as he drank in the sight of me in such a state.

Acting as if nothing unusual was happening, I walked over to him with a seductive sway of my hips. Softening my voice, I greeted him, "*Bienvenue à la maison, mon petit tout.*" Since I was significantly taller than him with my heels, I bent down to give him a sweet kiss to welcome him home.

He stared up at me, making fractured sounds of disbelief as he tried to make sense of my surprise.

"Let's get you out of these clothes." He didn't resist as I lifted his shirt off him, taking care to trail my fingers along his skin to send shivers through him. I slid his pants and briefs off him, enjoying copping a feel of his tight ass in the process before he kicked them aside. He may not have had words yet, but his prick was standing at full attention in appreciation of my surprise.

Lowering myself to my knees in front of him, I took off his socks for him. I gave him my best attempt at a demure look, careful to keep my voice soft for the illusion. "Does this please you?"

A squeak escaped him as he nodded, staring down at me with wide eyes. I reached behind him and ran my hands down his back to grope his ass and pull him closer.

I licked my lips as I looked up at him. "Do you wish for me to take care of you?"

"So much," he whispered in a strangled voice.

I leaned forward and pressed my lips to the underside of his cock, trailing teasing kisses with a hint of suction until I reached the tip. Letting it rest against my plump lips, I took my time sliding him into my mouth. Getting him nice and wet, I went down on him with great relish.

He grabbed onto my shoulder, gripping it so tightly that it almost hurt. His other hand found the back of my head, but he didn't use it to guide me. "Blessed holy mother of Saint Fuck, you're so beautiful!"

I rumbled in amusement low in my throat, earning me a swear as his hips jerked in response. Easing off him to recover, I then took him deeper, hollowing my cheeks as I bobbed along his length. To really push him to his limits, I reached behind him with my hand that wasn't holding his cock steady and teased his hole.

Staring up at him with lust, all it took to make him come undone was the hint of penetration as I swallowed around his length. He came with a loud gasp, so I drank down his release. I enjoyed making a show of licking him clean before I leaned back.

He sank to the floor as he stared at me in awe. "Iz—*what?*"

Taking his hand, I guided it to feel my arousal straining against the black lace boy shorts I had slipped on earlier. "Questions later. Pleasure now."

"Yes, Princess Goddess."

I helped guide him to get in bed, then slid out of the panties and kicked off my heels and joined him. He was putty in my hands as I prepared him to receive me. When we were ready to move on, it took a little fussing to position the voluminous tulle skirt over him.

Once I got settled, I started an easy rhythm as I rocked into him and built up the pleasure. The dress made it too hard to touch him, so I focused on holding his hips under it to help guide him as I chased my orgasm. Seeing him getting off on the fantasy of me dressed up like one of his anime girls meant it wouldn't take long for me to find release.

Pushing in deep, I called out his name as I came, thrusting until I was empty. I stayed still for a moment as I collected my bearings before I pulled out and moved back. To my surprise, he was rock hard again and staring up at me with pleading eyes.

Making sure my voice was gentle to maintain the girly illusion, I asked him, "What can I do to pleasure you more?"

"Jerk me off as you pretend like you're riding my cock? Please, Princess Divine."

"Anything for *mon petit tout*." I took care positioning myself over him. The full skirt made it easy to create the illusion that he was penetrating me while I gave him a hand job under it. I bounced and writhed like he was fucking me, making breathy sounds as I arched my back and begged him for more. Since I couldn't get off for real yet, I faked an orgasm to trigger his second climax. I kept pumping him until he was done, then held his gaze while I brought my hand up to lick off some of his cum. It earned me a strangled whimper that I savored.

Getting off him and staying in costume, I went to the bathroom to get a washcloth to clean him. When I finished, I sat next to him with my legs folded under me with the skirt spread out around me.

With effort, he rolled onto his side and marveled at me. "I love you so damn much, Princess Amazing. This was incredible." He played with the frilly skirt before tugging on it like he wanted me to come closer. I obliged him with a kiss. "It's amazing how you know me better than I know myself sometimes."

"*Pourquoi?*"

"Because I got so hung up on the traditional French maid fantasy, I never realized Japanese anime maid with pink hair was an option. And my god, you're even sexier than in my fantasies. I didn't think that was possible."

I smiled at him as I twirled one of the pigtails around my finger and released it with a bounce. "This seemed more in line with your aesthetic than a traditional maid costume. Plus, it's much cuter."

"And the black lace panties, thigh-highs, garter belts, and heels? Fucking hell, Princess Sin. I need to see you in just those."

His request didn't surprise me at all. "That can be arranged."

"You're so good to me." He gestured for me to lean down to kiss him. "Why do you even know how to walk in those?"

"Practice makes perfect."

His eyes fluttered closed as he pictured my rehearsals. "Fuck, you're sending my brain into overdrive with all this. I'm overwhelmed in the best of ways. You're amazing, and I love you so much. But also, fuck you for looking cuter in pink hair than me."

His playful reaction made me snicker. "*Non*, we must agree to disagree there. You look even more precious in that color."

"I'm borrowing your wig later to play with. It's too cute not to try on."

"As long as you let me watch."

He grinned up at me. "You kinky fucker."

"Surprise."

I laughed when he pulled me down into another kiss. My heart was full of love for my best friend, who gave my life so much meaning and vibrance. I would do anything to keep him laughing and smiling as we spent the rest of our lives together.

Epilogue

WREN

ONE MONTH LATER

DATING IZZY for real was *way* better than faking it. It also turned out that it wasn't too different from hanging out as friends; we just made out a lot more now and slept together, which was awesome.

After class, we headed to our favorite Brewhaha Café. Izzy liked them for their great coffee; I loved their chocolate chip muffins and whipped cream. It was a cozy, hole-in-the-wall kind of place, which had legendary status in our friend circle as being lucky. After all, it was where Callum and Rune had first met. You didn't get much luckier than that.

Because we were regulars, we had become friendly with the manager, Wolfie. That was his nickname, which I thought was hella appropriate given his wolfish grin. He had a wicked sense of humor, so joking with him whenever we visited was always fun. I also loved looking at him, because he was tall, gorgeous, and had the most beautiful amber-colored eyes that made him look like a wolf. Even in a simple white button-down shirt, jeans, and a black apron tied around his waist, he was stunning.

"Hey, guys!" Wolfie waved at us as we approached the counter. "How's it going?"

I wrapped my arms around Izzy and snuggled against him. We made quite the contrasting pair. I wore a baseball-style T-shirt with a cartoon cat grim reaper sparkling and exclaiming "Die." He was dressed impeccably in a fashionable blue paisley shirt with gorgeous red-and-gold detailing on the rolled-up cuffs that showed off his beautiful forearms. "Izzy's not just my best friend, but he's finally my boyfriend, too."

The news delighted Wolfie. "Really? That's great! Congratulations on making it official."

I beamed at him. "It's the best."

Izzy wrapped his arm around my shoulder and gave it a squeeze. "Indeed."

"I highly recommend falling in love with your best friend." It was too tempting to resist meddling a little. "Speaking of which, how's Eri doing? I haven't seen him here lately."

Wolfie snorted at my not-so-subtle attempt at bringing up his flirtatious relationship with his best friend. 'He's been busy with work."

"I can't imagine he's ever too busy to flirt with you." The two of them had a similar dynamic to mine with Izzy.

He scoffed at that. "I'm pretty sure being dead wouldn't stop him from flirting with me. He'd haunt me until I got a Ouija board so he could keep teasing me from the afterlife."

"It's even more fun when it's official. Seriously, you two should give it a shot."

"Nah, he's all about the chase. He doesn't want everything that comes after he captures me, trust me."

Izzy also seemed to notice the parallels between us. "I thought the same thing about Wren, but I couldn't have been more wrong."

"I talk a good game, but deep down, I just want to snuggle." I nuzzled against Izzy with a radiant smile.

Wolfie gave me one of his trademark half-grins. "I'm pretty sure you want to do more than *just* snuggle."

"Of course, but that was the thing I wanted most and was scared I'd never be allowed to have. And now that I can? It's fucking *awesome*."

He shook his head. "There isn't a world I can imagine where the two of us could do that without laughing at each other."

"Laughing makes it even more fun," Izzy assured him. "It is the benefit of being together with a friend, *non?*"

Wolfie shrugged. "Maybe if I'm not married by

the time I'm forty. Anyway, I'm assuming you want your usual?"

"Yep! I'm pretty sure it's sacrilegious to come here without eating a chocolate chip muffin with whipped cream."

"Brinley has turned so many people onto it, I'm talking to Early about adding it to the regular menu." Early was the café owner, who was sexy as hell and had an incredibly hot husband. They were another reason I was a repeat customer.

"You should! She's a culinary genius." Just like her brother, she was a lot of fun to joke around with, and her baking skills were second to none. It was always a bummer when she wasn't there to say hi to whenever we visited.

"I'll tell my sister you said that. It's totally going to make her day."

Izzy pulled out his wallet to pay since he loved spoiling me. "I'll also have my usual."

"Sure thing. Congrats again, guys."

I couldn't resist a parting shot. "I'll keep my fingers crossed for you and Eri."

He chuckled as he returned Izzy's credit card. "Thanks, but it'll take a lot more than that to make the impossible happen."

His reaction made me gleeful. "I can't wait to remind you of this conversation once you and Eri are together later."

He laughed and wished us a great rest of the day.

I left to get a table while Izzy waited for our order. The café was busy for that time of day, so I ended up near two hot guys who I normally would have been losing my mind over. Even sitting, you could tell the one with wavy sandy-blond hair, purple-rimmed glasses, and a long sweater vest over a white T-shirt was tall as hell. The other man with gray eyes and chestnut-colored hair made me laugh because he wore cut-up jeans with a T-shirt that said, "That's a horrible idea. What time?"

The guy in the funny shirt scrunched up his nose in an adorable way as he complained, "I'm sorry, but who calls a sexy cat boy *Boris*? Like, out of all the amazing names in the world, why would *anyone* choose a cheesy Russian mafia lackey for someone that cute? It makes no sense!"

The taller man chuckled before taking a sip of his drink. "What else would you expect from the people who turned Mad Hatter into Blood Dupre?"

It was rude to eavesdrop, but when they were talking about a Japanese series that I loved, I couldn't help it.

"It's just extra offensive with Cheshire is all I'm saying." He shrugged as he pulled off a piece of his chocolate chip muffin and ate it. Clearly, the man had excellent taste all around.

"And what would you call him instead?"

He pouted. "Why do we have to pick a different

name at all? What's wrong with just calling him Cheshire?"

I couldn't resist interjecting into their conversation. "Exactly! *Alice in the Country of Hearts* is great, but Boris Airay is a *terrible* name for the Cheshire cat. If it's supposed to be an *Alice in Wonderland* adaptation, why not leave the names the same so it actually feels like one?"

The man lit up at my agreement. "Thank you! See? This guy gets it! It's not just me being weird."

His partner shook his head ruefully. "You're acting like I disagree with you. It's definitely not the name I would have gone with."

It was a complaint I had harbored for a long time, so I couldn't resist piling on the argument. "If they wanted to do something different, why not pick a name that had CC as initials or some kind of anagram of Cheshire cat? Why *Boris*?"

"I don't have a clue," the taller man said with a shrug.

"Thanks for backing me up." The man in the T-shirt reached over to shake my hand. "I'm Jude, and this is my boyfriend, Rigby. He's getting his PhD in Japanese *Alice in Wonderland* adaptations, so I need all the help I can get to win that argument."

Rigby continued to look amused. "Again, I'm not disagreeing with you. There is no argument."

I stared at Rigby in shock. "Whoa, you can major in something like that? That's awesome!" It was almost as awesome as studying fuckology, which I still wished was a real thing.

Izzy returned with our drinks and my chocolate chip muffin that came with a generous mountain of whipped cream. "I see you're making friends."

I gestured at Rigby. "He's getting a PhD in Japanese *Alice in Wonderland* adaptations, which is awesome!"

Izzy took a seat across from me. "That sounds fascinating."

Jude looked at my plate with a quizzical expression. "Wait, did you get *whipped cream* for your chocolate chip muffin?"

Tearing off a piece and dunking it, I enjoyed my first bite. "Mm-hmm. It's *amazing*."

"I can honestly say I've never seen anyone eat a muffin with whipped cream before," Rigby said, side-eyeing my choice.

"It's not *that* weird when you think about it. People love whipped cream on chocolate chip pancakes, so chocolate chip muffins with whipped cream totally makes sense! If you ask Wolfie, I'm sure he'd give you some. Just tell him Wren recommended it to you."

Jude's eyes lit up with excitement. "Be right back!"

Rigby laughed as Jude dashed off to get some for himself. "When you put it that way, I'm shocked he's never tried it before. He's got quite the sweet tooth."

"You're missing out." I continued enjoying mine.

Jude returned with a plate piled high with

whipped cream and tried his muffin in it for the first time. He made a delighted noise at the delicious results. "Oh my god, this is the *best*! Seriously, try this." He nudged his plate with the muffin on it closer to his boyfriend.

Rigby obliged and sampled a taste. He nodded as he sucked the bit of whipped cream he had gotten on his finger. "Mm, that is good! I'm also impressed they make their own whipped cream instead of just using canned store-bought."

"Wolfie's sister helps him run the café," Izzy explained. "Brinley's a perfectionist who insists on everything being made from scratch. It's one of the many reasons this place is awesome."

Rigby hummed happily as he took another bite with a generous helping of whipped cream. "With food this good, how have I never heard of them before?"

"The Brewhaha Café is one of those 'it's your favorite place you've never been before' type of restaurants," I said. "It's one of Sunnyside's best-kept secrets."

"It's our first time here, but it won't be our last." Jude ate another bite of his treat. "Thanks for the recommendation."

"You're welcome!"

After that, we resumed our previous conversations with our partners. It gave me the chance to ask Izzy something that had been on my mind. "What are you doing during summer break?"

He took a sip of his coffee before answering. "I'm still debating my options. Why?"

"You always go to Paris to work with your brother over the summer, but he's here now. I just wondered if you'd be working with him."

"He's taking Felix to the Maldives for three weeks before they'll spend the rest of the summer in Paris together," Izzy replied.

I sighed in envy. "Wow, talk about living the dream. Felix is so lucky. Although Augie is going to lose his shit about his precious baby brother being gone so long."

Izzy chuckled, because we all knew how protective Augie was. "Brody is going to surprise Augie with a two-week Paris vacation to go visit Felix, so he'll be fine. Felix doesn't know about that, so it should be a fun surprise for them both."

"Wait, so if Arsène is going to be in Paris for summer break, what about you?"

"He may have requested I come work with him for a few weeks." Izzy shrugged as if it wasn't a big deal. "My parents would also like me to visit."

I tried not to feel sad that Izzy would have a fabulous summer vacation while I was stuck alone in our apartment, missing him like hell. "Oh."

He let the silence linger for an uncomfortable

amount of time as he took a long sip of his coffee. "They've also invited you as well."

My hopes suddenly rocketed sky-high. "Wait, really?"

He tried to hide his grin behind his mug, but I still saw it. "*Oui*, my parents are very excited to meet you." Since they were so busy with the vineyard, Izzy had always gone home to visit instead of them coming to Sunnyside.

"Holy Saint Fuck, this is amazing! Even if I have to sell stuff to afford buying a plane ticket, I'm going!"

"Oh, did I forget to mention we'll be flying first-class for free?" he asked in an airy voice.

My jaw dropped in shock. "I—what? *How?*"

"Since my brother travels all over the world for work, he has more air miles than he could ever use by himself. That means our tickets are free thanks to him, as is the upgrade to first class."

It was too much good news to contain my joy. I got up and threw myself on my boyfriend in a hug before kissing him passionately.

We broke apart when Jude made us laugh by cheering. "Now, *that's* how you celebrate!" He turned his attention to his boyfriend. "I don't suppose you're going to surprise me with news about us taking a summer trip to Japan together?"

Rigby adjusted his glasses, fighting back a smile. "Well, I *was* going to wait until your birthday, but—"

"Are we going to Japan? Please tell me we're going!"

He couldn't stop himself from grinning. "I found out yesterday I got the grant, so we're going to Tokyo, Kyoto, and Osaka."

Jude let out a whoop as he went over and gave his boyfriend the same kind of thank-you I just did. It was hot as hell, so I returned the favor of cheering for them. He said in between small kisses, "I love you so much." They both laughed when he stopped showering his boyfriend with affection. "Damn, this café is like the luckiest place on Earth. We're coming here all the time from now on."

"That sounds good to me," Rigby said as he looked at his boyfriend with deep love in his eyes.

Returning my attention to Izzy, I hugged him again. "Thank you, thank you, thank you! Other than finding out you were secretly in love with me, this is the best surprise ever!"

He reached up and brushed the hair from my eyes. "*De rien, mon petit tout*. I'd do anything to make you happy."

"Then you better take me straight home, because nothing would make me happier than celebrating with you naked, Prince Surprise."

He laughed at that. "After you're done with your muffin and chai."

Taking my seat so I could finish eating, my soul exploded into a starburst of radiant rainbows of happiness. Being madly in love with my best friend was the best thing that had ever happened to me. I had told him when we first met that I was the second luckiest man in the world. It was safe to say we were now tied for first.

Are Izzy and Wren ready to take their relationship to the next level? **Claim your copy of Prince Husband to find out today**.

Curious about Jude and Rigby's story? **Read Snowbody Like You to enjoy their swoon-worthy romance next**.

Want to see where the Sunnyside universe begins? **Check out Bet on Love to start the adventure**.

Thank You

Thank you for reading **Love Practice.** Reviews are crucial for helping other readers discover new books to enjoy. If you want to share your love for Izzy and Wren, please leave a review. I'd really appreciate it!

Recommending my work to others is also a huge help. Don't hesitate to give this book a shout-out in your favorite book rec group to spread the word.

About the Series

If you want to see more of Wren and Izzy's story, you can read an exclusive extra epilogue if you join my newsletter. It also includes a visual guide with the inspirational sexy pictures of Rune and Izzy from Arsène's show, so don't miss it!

If this was your first book in the **Good Bad Idea** series, you should check out **Bet on Love** to see where all the fun begins.

While this is the end of this series, this is not the last we'll be seeing of these guys. The **Good Bad Idea** characters will be putting in cameo appearances in all future books that take place in the Sunnyside universe!

The next Sunnyside series is **Suite Dreams**, which features men who fall in love at Luxurian Suites Hotels. Since it's part of the Sunnyside universe, it has the same tone, humor, and heat that you've come to expect from this series.

Snowbody Like You is the first book, which features Jude and Rigby from the epilogue. The meet-cute gods come through for them on a snowy day in an airport, leading to them being snowed in at a Luxurian Suites Hotel in a room with only one bed.

Once they return home to Sunnyside, their romance blooms into something truly beautiful and swoon-worthy. It's an insta love, role-playing, forced proximity, opposites attract, gay romance that will light your Kindle on fire while also hitting you right in the feels in the best way. It also features one of your favorite **Good Bad Idea** couples, so don't miss this one!

For you Armand fans, he's stars in the second book of the series, **Flawsome Explorations**. He finds an unexpected romance with Rigby's best friend and roommate. That means a bunch of the **Good Bad Idea** boys will be popping in for that one, so be sure to check it out!

Red the bartender, Wolfie the Brewhaha Café manager, and Wolfie's best friend Eri are all going to be featured in future Sunnyside series, so you haven't seen the last of them yet!

To stay up to date on the latest series news, please be sure to subscribe to my newsletter, follow me on Twitter and Instagram, or join my Facebook group, Ariella Zoelle's Sunnyside. I do exclusive previews every Teaser Tuesday and WIP Wednesday, so please come join us if you want a glimpse at what I'm working on for the future.

Next Release

AVAILABLE NOW

Jude longs to have a Hallmark meet-cute with the love of his life. But he learns how fun a happily ever after can be when he falls in love with a man whose imagination is as lively as his own.

Jude Moore

What's better than running into the love of your life in an airport while enacting a scene worthy of being in a Hallmark movie? That would be having the meet-cute gods snow us in together at a hotel with only one bed. Luckily, that's only the start of my incredible relationship with Rigby. There's so much more to our story because the *real* fun begins once we get home.

Falling for Rigby is easy because he's tall, adorable, and an academic nerd that makes my heart do the fandango. He's also a total sweetheart who knows how to make me swoon by indulging my wildest fantasies to make all of my wishes come true.

How could I not adore a man who gladly takes me on the trip of a lifetime to the Camelot of my dreams, where he's the romantic King Arthur to my Sir Lancelot?

Rigby Pasquali

I never thought I'd be the "fall in love at first sight" type, but Jude makes me believe in romance and a happily ever after. He's the first partner I've ever had who makes me feel safe enough to explore new sides of myself and discover what I want. When his creative imagination is as vivid as my own, it means there are no limits to the magical wonderlands we can create while we role-play scenarios that tick off *all* of the boxes on my wish list.

How did I get so lucky to end up with a boyfriend who can be everything I've ever desired and complete me in a way I never knew I needed?

Snowbody Like You is the first book in the ***Suite Dreams*** series and part of the Sunnyside universe. This novel features an insta love, role-playing, forced proximity, opposites attract, gay romance. If you love cute sweetness, sexy fun, and no angst stories that will make you laugh and swoon, you're going to love this satisfying HEA without cliffhangers. Each book can be read as a standalone or as part of the series in order.

Also by Ariella Zoelle

For a complete and up-to-date list of Ariella Zoelle's low angst releases, please visit her website at

www.ariellazoelle.com/ariella-zoelle-all

Also by A.F. Zoelle

In the mood for something with more angst and drama?
Check out A.F. Zoelle's dark romances at

www.ariellazoelle.com/af-zoelle-all

Acknowledgments

I can't even begin to tell you how grateful I am to all of you who took a chance on me and my **Good Bad Idea** series. I started 2020 off at one of my lowest points ever, so seeing the wild success of these books this past year has been a dream come true. It makes me even more excited to see where I'm going to be this time next year.

I've seen a lot of reviews say that these books feel like a warm hug from a good friend, which is one of the nicest compliments I've ever received. I'm so happy to know that they have comforted people during such a tumultuous year.

I've been so fortunate to become friends with my readers in my Facebook group. Amy Mitchell, Niki Cosgrove, Lindsay Porter, Tammy Jones, Lisa Klein, Kylie Anderson, and Vicki Cunningham are just a few who have truly touched my heart with their kindness and friendship over this past year. I feel truly blessed to have them in my life.

I also owe a huge thank-you to Katie from Gay Romance Reviews and all of their ARC readers. Before this series, nobody knew or cared about me or my writing. But thanks to their amazing efforts, they helped get my name out there so people could discover this series and fall in love with it. They've helped me reach an audience I never thought possible, which has changed my life for the better. To all of you who have left reviews, you've brought me that much closer to living the dream of leaving my job to write full-time. From the bottom of my heart, thank you.

I'll also never stop being grateful to Pam, Sandra, and Cate for helping me put my best foot forward when it mattered most. I'm so lucky to work with such talented people who have become friends this past year.

Quinn Ward has been the best mentor and friend I could have asked for. They've helped me reach incredible new heights and give me the courage to shoot for the moon.

I can't wait to meet again in **Snowbody Like You**!

About the Author

ariella zoelle
WWW.ARIELLAZOELLE.COM

Ariella Zoelle adores steamy, funny, swoony romances where couples are allowed to just be happy. She writes low angst stories full of heat, humor, and heart. But sometimes she's in the mood for something with a bit more angst and drama. If you are too, check out her A.F. Zoelle books.

Get a bonus chapter by using the QR code below!

Printed in Great Britain
by Amazon